DEATH BY DARK ROAST

A CHARLETON HOUSE MYSTERY

KATE P ADAMS

For Mum and Dad,
who brought me into a world full of books.

CHAPTER 1

There were delicate macarons in a rainbow of colours, chocolates with ingredients from chilli to lavender, and even bacon. Enormous wheels of cheese, fresh handmade doughnuts, pies and pastries. I found old-fashioned puddings that brought childhood memories rushing back, like sticky toffee and spotted dick. I saw at least three kinds of gin and multiple stalls selling honey, olive oils and chutneys. The list of locally produced mouth-watering foods went on and on.

One stall really stood out for me, though: 'Hayfield Haggis'. While many people looked down their noses at the dish made famous by the Scots, the traditional ingredients of oatmeal, liver, heart and lungs turning their stomach, I had already declared it as worthy of being my last meal, should such an occasion arise. In reality, most haggis no longer contains the more unappetising ingredients. Besides which, there are plenty more questionable items in things like hot dogs.

It doesn't need to be Burns Night for me to savour the heavenly haggis, and I'm not a whisky drinker so I bypass that tradition too. Haggis for me is a delicious treat at any time of the year, and now I had found a local farmer who had turned her hand to making it. Although it was yet to open to the public, as far as I was concerned the Charleton House Food Festival was already a resounding success.

Tomorrow was to be the first day of the festival and today the gardens were a hive of activity as stallholders set up their banners and displays. Over one hundred little white tents formed two circles around the Great Pond at the rear of the house, all of the action being watched over by two enormous lions that were part of the central fountain design. If visitors looked up from their artisan burgers or churros long enough, they'd witness it shooting fifty metres into the air.

The house gardeners were on hand, both to help stallholders and to make sure no one damaged the beautiful flowerbeds which had taken months to carefully prepare and nurture, so I had taken the opportunity to escape my endless to-do list and get a sneaky advance look at the delights that awaited my stomach and wallet. Food was one of my passions, that and history, and I had been able to combine the two perfectly when I was offered a job at Charleton House, a five-hundred-year-old stately home in glorious Derbyshire.

After a career in London, running cafés and restaurants that were frequented mainly by suited and booted City types, I was now the manager of three lovely visitor cafés at the house, and regularly catering dinners and events for the owners, the Duke and Duchess of Ravensbury – the heads of the Fitzwilliam-Scott family. Right now, today's visitors were being looked after by my teams, and I was enjoying the sunshine and teasing my taste buds with Mark, one of the house tour guides. I had been meant to meet someone else, but they had cancelled so I'd called Mark, and he hadn't thought twice before agreeing to join me to wander around the stalls, making ourselves hungry. Mark had taken me under his wing when I'd arrived almost a year ago and had quickly become a friend as well as my fount of all knowledge.

'It's looking good, Sophie.' Mark's eyes were practically out on stalks. He loved food as much as I did and was more than happy to be my official taster – and recipient of free pastries and coffees when I was feeling generous. 'There's a couple of ale stalls which I'll be checking out, and look! Raclette cheese grilled sandwiches. That's tomorrow's lunch sorted.'

The quickest path to Mark's heart was definitely through his stomach.

I had spotted my first choice for lunch within minutes of arriving when I'd seen the sign for a hog roast. I'd be sure my serving came with a mountain of crackling, the delicious, crisply roasted rind being my favourite bit.

'So who dared to cancel on you? Do they not realise how important and busy you are?'

I scowled and feigned annoyance at the healthy dollop of sarcasm in Mark's suggestion that I was anything other than rushed off my feet. 'Oh please, you were probably sitting in your office watching videos of cats online and hoping someone would call.'

'How dare you! It's dogs all the way for me.'

I laughed. 'Apologies, videos of puppies. It was one of my suppliers, Bruce from the Northern Bean Company. They supply our coffee. He said something about managing to get a last-minute appointment with someone in the area that he couldn't afford to miss out on. He sounded like he was in a foul temper, so I didn't mind not seeing him. Anyway, our meeting was just a check in, nothing important.'

'I thought you weren't keen on them?' Mark stretched his arm out to stop me walking into the path of a woman who was loaded up with enormous tubs of mustard and tomato ketchup, and not watching where she was going. Once she was out of the way, we set off again.

'I'm not. I'm seriously thinking about jettisoning them and finding another supplier, but that's going to be a difficult conversation so I don't mind delaying it by a day. I said I'd meet him tomorrow.'

'Tomorrow is often the busiest day of the week.' Mark had put on his best orator voice so I knew he was quoting someone.

'Who said that?'

'No idea. It's a Spanish proverb I think. Soph, over here. I know where we'll find you for the next three days.' I followed Mark until we were standing in front of a cherry-red VW campervan which had been beautifully transformed into a mobile coffee shop. Its roof had been raised so that staff could comfortably stand while working, the coffee equipment gleamed in the August sunshine, and shelves held bags of coffee beans and mugs that matched the colour of the van. The vision before me, combining my favourite colour with my favourite drink, was possibly the most stunning thing I had ever seen.

A young woman held up a remote control and the awning sprang to life, revealing red and white stripes. She was wearing a red t-shirt that matched the van, the sleeves rolled up revealing tanned, muscular arms. I guessed she didn't have any issues lugging around big sacks of beans.

'Nice, isn't it?' she said, smiling.

'Amazing, you've done an incredible job.'

'Can I get you a coffee?' With the awning in place, she jumped back into the body of the van. 'We roast our own beans.'

'Are you up and running? I don't want to get in your way.'

She made a start on the coffee, her movements quick and well-choreographed. There was no excessive banging like you'd hear in chain cafés; this was an art.

'It's all good to go, it doesn't take too much to set up. I'm Lucy Wright, and this is Kathy, my sister.'

A young woman with long, dark hair – a stark contrast to her sister's short blonde cut – appeared at the counter having popped up from the floor of the van and gave a little wave before disappearing again.

'Sophie Lockwood, I work here.' I pointed over my shoulder in the direction of the house. 'We've come for a sneaky peek.' As I said this, I realised that Mark was no longer beside me, having likely concluded that he was about to lose me to the bean that had an obsessive hold over my life.

I was handed a brown cardboard take-out cup that was emblazoned with a cherry-red logo saying 'Signal Box Coffee'. A little drawing of an old-fashioned railway signal box took pride of place in the centre. It was rather adorable, but I wondered about its significance.

It seemed that Lucy had spotted the question in my face. 'Our grandfather worked on the railways and had a replica signal box built in his garden. We used to play in it when we were kids. When he died, Kathy and I moved into the house and the signal box is where we roast the coffee.'

What a lovely story. As I took my first mouthful, I imagined how proud their grandfather would have been that his own interest was still playing a part in his grandchildren's lives in some way.

The coffee was rich and smooth. It was exactly the kind of pick-me-up that I enjoyed.

'Kenyan?' I looked at Lucy.

'Very good, yes.'

'I'm a bit obsessed with coffee and Kenyan AA is my go-to.' I took another mouthful, holding it there for a moment before swallowing. Only the best Kenyan beans were given an AA grade, the top tier of the country's grading system. 'This is particularly good. Nice and silky.'

'I have Kathy to thank for that, she's our buyer.'

Kathy had stepped out of the van by this point and reached out to shake my hand. She had a firm grip and her wrist was covered in dozens of small leather bands, a few brightly coloured string bracelets mixed in. They were all well-worn and looked like mementos of trips overseas.

She took over from her sister, filling me in on the company's operation. 'We might be a small business, but I wanted to make sure we had the best beans. I went to Kenya to learn as much as I could and this is what I came back with. Their growing conditions are fantastic. I'm glad you like it.'

Mark reappeared at my side and Kathy spoke to him as she started to move back towards the van. 'Would you like some?'

'No thanks. But I reckon you'll be seeing a lot of this one over the weekend' – he nodded in my direction – 'not that she needs help feeding her addiction.'

Kathy laughed. 'Well make sure you stop by whenever you need topping up.'

I thanked both Kathy and her sister, then steered Mark in the direction of more stalls.

We stepped carefully over trailing cables as the gardeners helped stallholders to connect to power supplies or hook up to enormous portable water tanks. There were still a number of vans arriving, their drivers trying to follow the map of the garden and figure out where they would be based for the duration of the festival. One vehicle in particular caught my eye: a large Airstream was being pulled into place by a Land Rover. The long silver bullet-like trailer had become all the rage a few years ago and was one of the coolest ways to explore the world, or your own back yard, but most people would need a second mortgage to be able to afford one of those things.

Demonstrating impressive skill, the driver reverse parked the trailer into position and three men jumped out of the Land Rover to start work on setting up. I checked out the writing on the side: 'Silver Bullet Coffee'. It looked like a slick operation. With well-practised ease, the workers propped the side of the van open, unfurled the canopy and started to transform the inside into a professionally presented coffee shop, albeit a little too modern and clinical looking for my taste.

A dark-haired man with the sleeves of his shirt rolled up caught my eye. 'Coffee?'

'Thanks, but I've just had one.' I held my coffee cup out to show him. 'Tomorrow, maybe?'

'Ah, the competition. Come on, just a taste. I have to make a few anyway, make sure everything's set up properly.' He spoke with confidence, like there was no question about my accepting a cup, not breaking eye contact with me until Mark spoke.

'Of course she will.' Mark stepped forward. 'The stuff is practically running through her veins at the best of times. I've yet to see her reach a limit. Plus she'll be so curious about it, she won't rest until she tries it.'

The man laughed, leaned over the counter and offered me his hand. He had a firm grip.

'Guy Glover, Silver Bullet Coffee. Nice to meet you both. Bear with me and I'll rustle a couple up.'

I stepped back and looked again at the van. 'This is quite the set up, you must be doing very well.'

'Thanks, we are. We've no shortage of bookings. We're particularly popular with music festivals – the young crowds love the trailer and we end up all over Instagram. It's great publicity.'

He looked a little too old to be spending time at festivals; not quite middle-aged, but no longer part of the 'young crowd' either.

'We're not always so keen on the music, though,' another member of the team grumbled through a smile as he carried a box past us. 'I swear my ears are still ringing after that last one.'

Guy chuckled. 'Yeah, he got stuck next to a rock stage last weekend. Sadly I couldn't be there to help out.'

'Sadly? You couldn't find an excuse fast enough.' The man carrying the box raised an eyebrow. He had a warm smile and appeared to be enjoying the banter with Guy. His Silver Bullet t-shirt was clinging to his body with sweat and he shook his head to get his hair out of his eyes. I avoided looking at Mark; I imagined his mouth hanging open as he pictured the slim, healthy-looking man minus the t-shirt.

Guy introduced us. 'This is Ben. You might need to shout to get his attention until his hearing returns to normal.'

We introduced ourselves and took the coffee Guy was offering to us. Mark was right: I couldn't recall ever having turned down a cup. Guy watched as we took our first sips; it was a bit too hot, but I nodded my approval as I had a second taste.

'It's good. Nutty, nice after-taste.'

'Here,' Guy handed over a small bag of beans, 'take some with you, but be sure to come back and see us over the weekend.' A third man had joined Guy and acknowledged me with a nod. 'That's Kyle, my business partner.'

Kyle looked as if he'd just got out of bed and needed a coffee more than any of us. I returned his nod, then turned back to Guy, thanking him. As we walked away, Mark bent down and whispered conspiratorially in my ear.

'Go on, spill the beans, so to speak. What did you really think of their coffee? You weren't exactly bubbling over with enthusiasm.'

'Ha, you know me too well. Pedestrian at best. It was OK, but not very complex. It tasted no different to the dark roast we serve in the cafés and you know I'd love to replace that with something more interesting.' I'd been so unimpressed with the coffee when I first arrived at Charleton House that I'd taken to keeping a stash of my favourite beans tucked away in a filing cabinet in my office, and I rarely touched the coffee we sold to the visitors.

As I mulled over the similarities between what I had just tasted and what I sold in the cafés, a weight slammed into my shoulder. I staggered into Mark, who managed to keep me upright as pain shot through my arm. It was as if I'd been hit by a truck.

As I steadied myself, I turned to see who had almost knocked me off my feet. A man in a gardens team t-shirt and baseball cap was striding with purpose towards the Airstream and clearly nothing was going to get in his way. I watched as he grabbed Ben's arm and swung him round to face him. Either I was too far away or the gardener was keeping his voice down, but I couldn't hear what he was saying. However, I could see that his face had an expression of fury chiselled into it, and whatever he was saying to Ben wasn't pretty and was probably delivered with a ton of angry spittle. Ben was saying nothing, just looking shocked.

As quickly as it had happened, it was over. The gardener spun round and marched back the way he had come, his face red, his hard eyes staring ahead. His fists were clenched into tight balls as though he was trying to control an urge to use them. Despite coming close enough for me to hear his ragged breathing, he didn't appear to see me and didn't apologise for having barged into me.

I turned to look at Ben, who was watching the man walk away. Then with a look of resigned sadness, he shook his head and slowly carried on with his work.

'Are you OK?' I looked up at Mark and nodded. He was staring at the angry gardener's retreating back. 'Remind me never to annoy him; I'd hate to see those fists get some action. Come on, Soph, let's go.'

Mark put an arm around my shoulders and we crunched our way up the gravel path towards the house.

CHAPTER 2

Charleton House is, from the outside at least, a glorious show of Baroque opulence and power, and could easily be mistaken for a royal palace. When the sun glints off its gilded window frames, it's easy to imagine generations of family members looking out onto manicured lawns, colourful planting and delicately sculptured topiary, the gardens providing a restful break between plotting political takeovers and attempts to cosy up to the reigning monarch. The honey-coloured sandstone building has been the home of the Fitzwilliam-Scott family for over five hundred years, its 300 rooms bearing witnesses to history of both the romantic and scandalous kind. This weekend, the current Duke and Duchess would be using the magnificent house as a backdrop against which to showcase some of the finest food in the area, and I was like a kid at Christmas. I was going to need regular reminding that I was here to work and not just eat and drink my way through the three-day weekend.

Mark and I took a short cut through a door marked 'Private', making our way into the house and down a flagstone corridor. We cut across a courtyard that looked distinctly different from the rest of the building, as it and the ground floor rooms around it dated back to the original Tudor house, and gradually wound our way to the Library Café and my office.

The Library Café is my favourite of the three cafés I am responsible for, although I'm sure that, like parents with more than one child, I should never admit to having a favourite. As the name suggests, it's decorated and furnished to look like the luxurious library of one of the earlier Dukes. Hundreds of books line the shelves that cover every wall; armchairs you could sink into rest in front of a large, ornate fireplace; tables of different sizes and shapes fill the rest of the room. It is popular with staff who want to hold meetings outside their office, or bring paperwork and escape their phones and emails, as well as visitors in search of lunch and a chance to rest their feet.

Today, the dark space was refreshingly cool after we'd been spending so much time in the heat of the garden. Mark plonked himself down in the nearest armchair and I sat on the arm of one opposite, not wanting to get too comfortable. My day was far from over.

Mark let out an exaggerated sigh. 'The diet's off, then, or at least delayed. I couldn't see a food stall that wasn't tempting.'

'Diet?' Wide-eyed, I looked him up and down. 'You're stick thin as it is. I'm trying to fatten you up with as much cake as possible, but I think you've got worms.'

'That was what my mother used to say. As a kid, I'd stand in front of cupboards and "graze", as she called it, but it never made any difference.' He shrugged his shoulders in mock defeat. 'Don't stop trying, though, I'm sure the cake is helping in some way.'

'Sophie, sorry to disturb.' Tina, the supervisor who looked after the Library Café for me, appeared by my side. 'Terry is here.'

'Thanks, Tina, tell him I'll be right out.'

'Who is this Terry?' enquired Mark, turning his head to give me a sly look. 'Is he a thing of beauty that you've been hiding from me?'

'Terry Mercer is a short, bald twenty-two-stone culinary

11

genius who owns an award-winning restaurant in Sheffield and is catering tonight's event. He's not my type and I have no idea if I'm his. So you can curb that imagination of yours. I need to help him set up. Be off with you.' I waved my arms in the direction of the door as though I was shooing out a cat. It had the desired effect and Mark got up to leave. Sadly, he didn't get far before the leather-clad figure of Detective Constable Joe Greene walked in.

When I first started working at Charleton House almost twelve months ago, Joe was coming to the end of his time as a motorcycle police officer whose bike was regularly parked up outside the security office while he conducted 'important police business', also known as eating his way through my profits, in one of the cafés. Now, he was a plainclothes detective constable, but he didn't seem to spend any less time dropping by the house. He was also Mark's brother-in-law, so we were party to more local gossip than was probably legal. Between Joe and me, we playfully kept Mark on his toes.

Today Joe was in his own bike leathers and appeared to be on his way home.

'Ello, 'ello, 'ello,' was Mark's version of a welcome. 'Here to arrest me, officer?'

'Society should be so lucky,' Joe replied quickly. If anyone could give Mark as good as they got, it was Joe. 'It's pretty much the weekend, give or take, so I was wondering if you two were free to get it started with a visit to the pub?'

'Sorry, chaps' – I shook my head – 'you're on your own. I'm working the Food Festival drinks reception. Have a drink for me, though.'

'I'm up for it.' Mark made his way over to his brother-in-law. 'I'm not going on the back of the bike, though. I consider myself highly adventurous of mind and spirit, less so of body.'

'I couldn't risk you raising the centre of gravity anyway.'

Joe and I both laughed. It was funny to imagine Mark's tall, skinny frame sticking upright like the mast of a ship, while Joe crouched over the handlebars of his powerful sports bike. It was even funnier to imagine Mark carefully squeezing his perfectly groomed handlebar moustache under a motorcycle helmet without damaging it.

'I'll head home, drop off the bike and change, then I'll get a taxi so I can have a drink. See you there in an hour?'

Mark turned towards me just as I was rearranging my hair in the glass of a framed picture on the wall. I wanted to look my best for tonight's event, but I was short on time so I checked that my artistically ruffled short hair hadn't gone flat in the heat.

'I hate to be the one to tell you, Sophie, but you've got a few grey hairs coming through.'

I gave Mark a hard stare, trying not to laugh. Not only was I entirely grey but, despite me only being in my forties, the majority of it was already turning silver.

'Idiot!' Joe smacked Mark on the back of the head with one of his gloves. 'That's no way to talk to a lady.'

'Lady?' Mark exclaimed. 'Since when has she...' Joe hit him again. I laughed out loud.

'To be fair, I've never claimed to be at all ladylike...'

The banter was interrupted by the sound of Joe's phone. 'DC Greene... Hey, Julie, what's up?... That's right, off for a pint... Oh, OK, I guess not. I'll head straight there, thanks.' Joe finished the call and looked forlornly at Mark. 'Sorry, you're drinking alone. Looks like I'm not off duty after all. There's been a theft up at Berwick Hall.' Nine-hundred-year-old Berwick Hall was another magnificent historic building that was open to the public, about thirty minutes' drive from Charleton.

'What's happened? Nothing serious, I hope.'

'A painting's been stolen from a public area. No one noticed it was missing until they were closing up for the day, so I can only assume it wasn't some enormous portrait. Either that or a visitor was carrying the world's biggest handbag. I better head off. Are you going to the pub anyway, Mark? I might be able to catch up with you later.'

'I'd like to. I'll see if Bill wants to join me, turn it into a date night.' Built like the ex-professional rugby player he was, Bill was the opposite of his skinny husband, and always enjoyed challenging stereotypes with his tough, no-nonsense broken-nosed looks.

Joe walked out the door, calling, 'Hope to see you and my big brother later, then, Mark,' over his shoulder. Time was ticking and I knew I had to get on. I packed Mark off to the pub, grabbed my notebook and went to find Terry; I'd already left him waiting too long.

CHAPTER 3

*T*he Library Café kitchen looked out onto a lane that was out of bounds to visitors. Here staff took short cuts, deliveries were made, and it was where the security office was based. There were always people coming and going, but when an event was being set up, it became a hive of activity. You had to be careful to make sure you didn't get hit by distracted people carrying furniture, trip over cables for lighting, or get run over by trolleys piled high with food or bottles of wine.

This evening's event was pretty small and relaxed in comparison to some of those held within the more decadent rooms of the house. There would be no ballgowns or tuxedos, but there was still plenty to do. I'd collected Terry from his van on the lane and was walking him through to the Gilded Hall, a magnificent room with a grand staircase ideal for making speeches and representing the grandiosity of the house. The ceiling was home to a brilliant Baroque mural by Antonio Verrio, a favourite of kings and queens. The staircase, a grand carving of alabaster, marble and the local mineral Blue John, led up to a balcony that ran the full length of the south side of the room. Every inch of the elaborately decorated railing was covered in gold leaf, hence the name of the room. There was no doubting the wealth and status of the Fitzwilliam-Scott family throughout the centuries. It was an awe-inspiring space which could hearten or intimidate you, depending on your frame of mind and the tone of the event you were attending.

'So the canapés will be served in here?' Terry asked.

'Yes, canapés and champagne in here. The Duke will make a speech, thank the main sponsors, then mingling will take place while the string quartet plays. At the same time, small groups will be taken off on short tours of the state rooms. The whole thing will be done and dusted by 8pm. Nice and simple.'

'That's easy for you to say' – Terry rubbed his hand over the top of his head – 'you're used to this place. I followed all the food guidelines, but I'm still terrified that something I made will stain the floor if it gets dropped.' All caterers were told what could and couldn't be served in order to help protect the historic environment and objects, so no greasy or highly coloured foods. If guests were going to be standing, then they were limited to clear drinks such as champagne, white wine and water.

'You'll be fine; you've had everything checked over. If our event manager is happy then you're good to go.' As if on cue, the Charleton House event manager, Yeshim, arrived, a little flustered and tucking her shirt in as she ran across the room.

'Sorry, sorry, I was stuck on the phone with a supplier. Everything OK, Terry? You look terrified! Don't worry, your food is great, and the Duchess loves your restaurant. Thanks for looking after him, Sophie, I'll take over from here.' Yeshim had incredible energy levels and rarely seemed to take a breath. She was great fun to work with, but exhausting company. I usually made sure I had an enormous mug of coffee with me when I joined her for meetings.

Even though I wasn't catering this event, I'd offered to help out. As a relatively new member of staff, I took every opportunity to learn how the place ran. I was also still in the starry-eyed stage of my career at Charleton where I'd happily sacrifice a Friday night to work, even if it wasn't necessary.

The event was starting to take shape. The string quartet had arrived and was setting up in an alcove at the bottom of the stairs. An electrician was adding a few additional lights and making the room feel a little more dramatic, not that it took much. Ellie Bryant, a member of the conservation team, hovered in the background, making sure no one did anything that could cause any damage. She might resemble a waif-like creature who would prefer to disappear into the background, but I have witnessed Ellie launch herself at a teenager who, for a bet, had clambered over a rope and made himself comfortable in a an eye-wateringly beautiful gilt wood armchair designed by William Kent for the Third Duke in the eighteenth century. Ellie was passing in time to see his bottom reach the padded seat covered in a navy blue damask and gave him a verbal dressing down which probably left him in therapy for years.

A group of tour guides made their way upstairs, ensuring that the rooms they planned on taking guests through didn't hold any surprises, the paintings they would be talking about were still in place, and nothing had been removed for cleaning or loaned to exhibitions. I pictured my favourite tour guide, Mark, in the Black Swan, enjoying a pint of local ale and a mountain of fish and chips while I would be spending the next hour helping to line up 150 wine glasses, passing the electrician his tools, finding some safety pins to help a waitress secure her skirt after the zip had broken, and fetching a plumber to unblock a toilet. It was a good job I didn't aspire to a life of glamour.

Eventually, calm descended alongside a gentle air of anticipation. Being as this was such a small event, none of us were on edge. Occasions like this gave us the chance to savour our surroundings almost as much as the guests did.

As the guests started to arrive, serving staff offered champagne round, the bottles having been opened in a back corridor to avoid flying corks damaging precious artwork. The Duke and Duchess worked the room, welcoming everyone in their usual down-to-earth fashion and thanking them for their support. Terry's canapés were clearly a hit, and I watched as a couple of the guests cut across the room and homed in on a server who was carrying their favourite little taste bomb to grab a few more. Honey coloured lighting glinted off gilt mirror frames and the string quartet sent waves of Beethoven out across the gradually filling room.

'So far, so good.' I jumped as Yeshim appeared by my side. 'Terry finally calmed down, with the help of a glass of champagne, but I'm going to have to keep an eye on him. It went down far too quickly. The last thing we need is him sliding down the banisters as the Duke makes his speech. There he is.' She pointed across the room to a slightly wobbly looking Terry. 'And yes, there's another glass of champagne in his hand.'

I looked over in time to see Terry exchange an empty champagne glass for a full one as a server with a tray of drinks walked by.

'Oh no, there's the Duchess, and she's joining him.' Standing beside Yeshim was like having my own private sports commentary, and I wasn't sure I could get a word in if I tried. 'No, he's not... he won't... he has.' Yeshim let out a loud, exasperated sigh as Terry put his arm round the Duchess's waist and laughed far too loudly at something she said. Like a bird of prey, Yeshim swept in, had a quiet word in the Duchess's ear and steered her away from Terry's grasp, no doubt having thought of someone she could claim it was important the Duchess meet.

Well done, Yeshim.

As I scanned the party, my eyes rested on a man in a dark suit talking to the Duke and gesturing around the room. It was Detective Inspector Mike Flynn, who had got wind of my involvement in police business during the summer and wasn't my biggest fan. I wasn't surprised to see him here. Joe had told me just how ambitious Flynn was, and cultivating a friendship with someone as important as the Duke was no doubt part of the plan to help him shoot up the ranks.

DI Flynn scanned the room until his eyes came to rest on me. He raised his glass of champagne in my direction, but the expression on his face remained indifferent. It looked as if we wouldn't become friends anytime soon.

A hush came over the crowd and I noticed that the string quartet had stopped playing. Yeshim was talking to the Duke at the bottom of the stairs. A broad-shouldered, tall and handsome man, he had the stature and presence of one of the stags that roamed the Charleton estate. Wearing a navy blue pinstriped suit that was perfectly tailored to his figure, his pale-blue shirt open at the collar, he'd chosen to go without a tie. He cut a classical figure that matched his exquisite surroundings: a man of power, influence and style.

The Duke climbed halfway up the stairs, where he turned and waited patiently for silence to descend. With a charming, welcoming smile, he scanned the room.

'Ladies and gentlemen, it is such a pleasure to welcome you all to Charleton this evening. My wife and I gain so much joy from sharing this wonderful house with others and I thank you all for joining us. The Charleton Food Festival is one of my personal highlights of the year, and here in Derbyshire we are fortunate to have some of the country's finest artisan producers. This is a fabulous opportunity for them to showcase their talents, and we are so grateful to you, our many sponsors, for helping to make this possible...'

As the Duke spoke, my mind started to wander. It wasn't that he was a poor public speaker; just the opposite, in fact. He was an accomplished speech writer, and although his cut-glass accent was a throwback to more socially divided times, with the Duke it was just another part of his charming and gentlemanly image rather than an attempt to make his audience feel that they were in the presence of someone superior to them. But I'd heard him speak on many previous occasions and this was a fairly run-of-the-mill event, so I was able to tune out what he was saying.

I found myself wondering about the gardener who had barged into me earlier in the day, and I instinctively rubbed the spot on my arm where we'd collided. I was bound to have a bruise by now. It was a long time since I'd seen someone look quite so angry; he had been a rather frightening figure as he'd barrelled past Mark and me. Whatever Ben had done, it must have been pretty awful.

My thoughts were interrupted by laughter as the crowd reacted warmly to something the Duke had said.

'...So please, help me prove my wife wrong, just once.' He smiled in the direction of the Duchess who was laughing at his comments. 'Now, please enjoy the champagne and delicious food, take one of the tours with our extremely knowledgeable guides and have a lovely evening. Thank you again for all of your support.' He raised the champagne glass he had been cradling in his hand, smiled and slowly nodded his appreciation. His words were met with rapturous applause, and as he descended back into the crowd, the string quartet began to play again.

'I've never seen him fail to capture an audience.' A deep voice came from over my right shoulder and I turned to see a smiling ruddy-faced man. Wearing a checked shirt and tweed jacket, he looked as if he'd just come in from a hunt. 'Malcolm,' – he offered me his hand – 'Malcolm De Witt. I was up at Oxford with the Duke. He was forever jumping on tables to make speeches after a drink or two. It's good to see he's calmed down a little from his student days.'

'Sophie, I work here. You're a friend of the family?'

'I was. We're just getting reacquainted after a few years in the friendship wilderness. No one's fault, adult life just gets in the way. We used to ski together every year when the children were young, ran into each other at a university alumni event a couple of months ago and he invited me to stay for the week as I was due to be in the area on business.' Malcolm had a far off look in his eyes, like he wasn't fully engaging with me but just wanted to kill the time with someone – anyone. He was nice enough, though.

'Have you been here before?'

'Many times. A gang of us used to come up for a month every summer while we were students, got up to all sorts of mischief. Then there was the occasional Christmas party. Once his father died and Alex became Duke, he got too busy and my work took me overseas so we lost touch.' He was watching as the Duke entertained a group of fawning ladies who were gathered around him like twelve-year-olds around a pop star. 'Look at him. We're exactly the same age, give or take a week or two, and yet he looks twenty years younger than me. I, on the other hand, am carrying every single one of my sixty years.' He patted his stomach. 'Well, we only get one go around, may as well enjoy it. Lovely chatting, Sophie, I'm sure I'll see you again.' He drained his champagne glass, and with that, he was off, homing in on some bite-sized cheesecakes that were being offered to the guests.

'Sophie?' I had just said goodbye to Yeshim, who I had agreed could have an early night. I was more than capable of overseeing the end of the drinks reception. 'Sophie, I need to talk to you.'

Domenico Negri was trying to get my attention. Despite Negri being over 200 years old and long since dead and buried, this wasn't as crazy as it sounds. A couple of members of the live interpretation team had been employed to attend the reception dressed as significant food-related characters who had links with the house and engage with the guests. During the day, they would dress as historical characters and talk to the visitors, often recreating events from throughout the history of Charleton House. They weren't simply actors who memorised lines and hoped no one asked them an awkward question; they carried out in-depth research and took pride in remaining in character, no matter what they were asked or how visitors behaved around them.

Negri had been an Italian confectioner who, in the 1760s, had supplied the 5th Duke of Ravensbury with a spectacular dessert for his wife's birthday. Negri had presented an enormous, delicately handcrafted spread of sweetmeats, macarons, biscuits, marshmallow, fruits and creams, which would have been displayed like a work of art with sugar ornaments creating country scenes, fountains and buildings.

I took Negri over to a quiet corner.

'What's wrong?'

'It might be nothing. I might just have missed it, but I don't think so.' The Italian accent he had been using with the guests had gone. I rested my hand on his arm.

'What might you have missed? I don't understand.'

Negri took a deep breath, glanced around, then carried on, almost whispering.

'I was walking through the Stone Gallery. I know it's not officially open tonight, but we've been allowed to use it to get from our changing room to here. Well, I've been back and forth a couple of times, but when I came back through it a few minutes ago, I noticed that something was missing. Do you know the big green bowl with a brown rim? Looks like chocolate has been smeared round the edge and is melting into the bowl? It always sits on the table below the painting of the girl and dog?' His description rang bells, but I honestly couldn't be sure I knew what he was referring to. 'I could have sworn it was there earlier in the night, but now it's gone. The table is empty.'

My heart sank. I had dealt with drunken guests and fire alarms, running out of wine, and guests and staff alike being taken ill, but never this. Now I wished I hadn't let Yeshim go home. I called the security office on the radio and let them know we had a possible missing object, then searched around for the conservation team member who had been keeping an eye on things. When I found her, I pulled her aside.

'Ellie, quick, I need you to come with me.'

'What's wrong?'

'Not here.' I led her out of the room, trying to look calm and composed, and took her through to the Stone Gallery, a simple stone-floored corridor where some of the Duke's art was on display. Beneath the picture of a girl and a dog stood an empty table.

'Is there normally a bowl here?' I asked.

'Yes,' – she looked confused – 'the St Ives Bowl. Where is it?'

'I was hoping you could tell me. It's not gone for conservation work or been loaned out?'

'No, we never loan it out. It's a personal piece of the Duke's, a gift to his mother by the ceramicist who made it. It has no financial value, but he loves it.' The Dowager Duchess had been a real firebrand: a remarkable character who loomed large over the more recent history of Charleton House. It was she and her husband the 11th Duke of Ravensbury, who had first opened the house to the public. Glamorous, outspoken and possessed of a wicked sense of humour, she was rarely seen without a martini in her hand in her later years, and martini would always be found on the Garden Café menu in her honour. I wished that she had lived long enough for me to meet her; I know I would have been terrified of her, but in awe of her nonetheless.

Ellie glanced around, as though expecting to find the bowl on another shelf or above one of the fireplaces along the wall.

'What's going on, girls?' I recoiled at the use of 'girls', but chose to ignore it and turned to face Pat, a security officer.

'We're missing a bowl.' I pointed at the table. 'It was there at the start of the evening, now it's gone.'

Pat thought for a moment. 'You positive?' He looked at me like I was a small child. 'Sure you're not mistaken, mislaid it, your memory going?'

'Very sure.' My teeth were clenched. I took a deep breath and spoke slowly and clearly. 'I'm reporting a missing item to you. I trust I can now leave this in your hands and...'

'Is everything alright?' Before I had the chance to start using four-letter words, DI Flynn walked in. 'I saw security come through.' He nodded at Pat. 'Can I be of assistance?'

'A significant item from the collection has gone missing, sir.' Pat stood ramrod straight, his voice having changed to one of control and respect. He seemed determined to make me punch him this evening. 'I was just about to take appropriate action when you walked in, sir.'

I stepped forward, glaring at Pat as I did so, daring him to stop me carrying out my role. As onsite manager for the event, I quickly filled DI Flynn in on the situation and that we were about to call the police.

'Well, as the police are already onsite' – the corner of his mouth showed the beginnings of a smile – 'I'll take over.' He nodded at Pat. 'You head back to the security office and get your team to start shutting this place down. I don't want anyone leaving. I'll have a quick word with the Duke, break the news to him. All clear?'

'Absolutely, sir.' Pat dashed off down the corridor, looking as if it was the first time he'd done any 'dashing' in years and he was probably regretting the family-sized pizza I'd seen him ploughing his way through earlier in the evening.

DI Flynn turned back to us. 'I'll need everyone to remain onsite, so please let your teams know. Now if you'll excuse me, I need to break the news to the Duke.'

With that, he strode purposefully down the corridor, and I prepared to spend the rest of the evening placating guests who were trapped here. Mind you, there were worse places to be trapped.

.   .   .

Fortunately, the majority of the guests didn't notice that there was a problem. We just kept pouring wine, and when we were out of canapés, I ran back to the Library Café kitchens and pulled a few cakes out of the fridge. Alcohol and cake – it was a sure-fire way to keep people occupied and onside.

In the meantime, the Stone Gallery had been closed off and declared a potential crime scene. DI Flynn, with the help of the security team, had conducted a sweep of nearby rooms to check the bowl hadn't found its way elsewhere, and all the live interpreters who had used the gallery as a short cut had been put in a separate room. When I'd taken them some refreshments, I'd been met by a bizarre sight: two eighteenth-century characters, one male, one female, sitting on a very modern sofa, killing time on their mobile phones. It wasn't an unfamiliar sight, but it never failed to amuse me.

After a thorough search of staff bags, eventually DI Flynn declared that the reception guests could leave, but anyone with a bag large enough to conceal the bowl would need to be searched. Once the guests had gone, he pulled me aside.

'I just wanted to give you a quick update. The Stone Gallery is off limits and I have a team in there now, taking fingerprints. We've completed bag searches and found nothing, so we'll let the staff leave shortly. There's currently no sign of anything on CCTV, and the likelihood is that the bowl is long gone.' He sighed. 'The Duke is of course devastated, but equally he's realistic about it all, especially with the lack of any sort of art alarm system attached to the item. I was rather hoping that he would have invested in some upgrades to the security system by now, especially after recent events.'

He was referring to a murder that had occurred onsite a couple of months ago. Much to DI Flynn's annoyance, I had identified the killer before anyone else. This event was the first time our paths had crossed since the murder and I was a little surprised by how civil he was being, but I took it as a sign of his professionalism and gave him a brownie point.

'Do you think this is related to the theft up at Berwick?'

'I don't know, but it seems a bit of a coincidence that something goes missing from two historic buildings not far apart on the same day.' He paused, then looked at me intently. 'But what I do know is that the police don't need any help.' His eyes drilled into mine. 'OK?'

I nodded. 'The thought had never crossed my mind, Inspector.'

CHAPTER 4

I'd been warned that the cafés would be quiet over the weekend of the Food Festival, but my staff weren't allowed to take it easy. When I arrived at work the next morning, I helped to set up the Garden Café, a beautiful Baroque orangery with enormous ceiling-high windows that looked out onto the gardens. When it was built in the 1700s, it had been heated with stoves, and in the winter it was used as a conservatory for delicate plants. Now it was an elegant café where visitors came for afternoon tea and a glass of champagne. When the British weather was behaving itself, the doors were fastened back and tables placed among the lime and lemon trees that decorated the patio.

Most of my team had yet to arrive so I had the opportunity to enjoy my surroundings in peace. The sunlight streamed in and cast a gauze-like veil over the tables. The glassware had been polished to within an inch of its life and sparkled, ready to hold fine wines, glasses waiting to be clinked together in moments of celebration. The freesias that had been delivered by the gardens team were ready to go in delicate vases and bring some subtle colour to each table.

'Morniiiing,' Mark trilled as he flew through the door. 'The sun is shining, you need more coffee and I need gossip, so we're heading out to the garden where you can fill up on caffeine and loosen that tongue of yours.' He put his arm through mine and marched me towards the patio doors that were already open. We let ourselves out through a gate and made our way down the path towards the Food Festival stalls.

There was already a buzz of activity, even though it was only 9am. It was still an hour until the visitors would be let in, but there was bound to be plenty to do before then. Robin Scrimshaw, the head gardener, was heading in the same direction as us with an enormous roll of black bin bags under his arm.

'Bit early, aren't ya?' he asked.

'We reckoned we could have a bit of a wander before the hordes arrive,' Mark replied. 'Besides which, if I don't get some good quality coffee in this one, then... well, it's just not worth thinking about.'

I smiled and shrugged in agreement. 'Will you get a chance to explore the stalls?' I asked Robin.

'Sort of. The whole garden team is being kept busy, whether it's emptyin' bins' – he pointed at the bin bags under his arm – 'or keeping people off the flowers, but we always get given treats by the stallholders for free, especially if we help 'em out with somethin.'

We'd reached the circle of stalls and Robin set off to distribute rubbish bags. Lucy and Kathy were still setting up Signal Box Coffee. The cherry-red van immediately put a smile on my face, and Lucy spotted me straight away.

'Morning, Sophie, can we get you a coffee?'

'That would be great, thank you.'

'And...' She looked at Mark.

'Mark. I'd love some, thank you.'

As Lucy got to work, I spotted Kathy carrying some boxes

into the van. She nodded in our direction when she saw us, but she looked tired and not quite as happy to be there as her sister.

'So, how did the Duke take it?' Mark brought me back to last night's events. 'He must have been furious to have it taken right from under his nose.'

'It wasn't exactly under his nose. It was hard to tell, he seemed quite business-like. Maybe "subdued" would be the right word. When I saw him, he was just listening to DI Flynn as he updated him.'

Mark shook his head. 'Poor man, he loves that piece. The previous Duchess cherished it, and so did he once his mother passed away.'

'If it was so precious, why was it on display in a public route? Why didn't he keep it in his study or somewhere off limits?'

'The artist became quite well known, and when she died, the Duke felt it was important to share her work with the public. That's just the way he is. He doesn't believe art should be locked away and enjoyed only by those with vast amounts of money. Also, it doesn't have a great deal of financial value. The artist became recognised as a superb ceramicist, but she wasn't hugely collectable. So in theory, it wasn't at risk.'

'Then why would someone steal it if it's not valuable?' I asked. Mark shrugged his shoulders.

'No idea. The thrill? The mistaken belief that it was valuable?'

'Here you are, two mugs of coffee. You can keep the mugs.' Lucy had appeared with two wonderful Signal Box Coffee mugs; they were the classic chunky diner shape and mine felt great in my hand. A little illustration of a signal box and the name of the company were painted on the side in white; the mug itself was a red that matched the van.

She had made my morning. 'Thanks, Lucy, they're great,' – I took a sip – 'and so is the coffee. I held off having my usual cup when I got to work; I wanted to wait for this.' I breathed in the rich aroma and took a bigger mouthful. Lucy looked over at Mark and smiled.

'Sorry, did you have to suffer while she deprived herself of caffeine?'

'She wasn't too bad, but I keep a taser to hand just to be on the safe side.' He smirked, clearly delighted that he'd found someone to engage with in some banter at my expense.

'Don't encourage him. It was worth the wait. Look, I've been thinking, I'd love to sit down with you sometime and learn a bit more about the company.'

I was about to suggest we catch up once the festival was over when I was interrupted by a voice in my ear. 'Ours is much better.'

I turned quickly and spilt hot coffee on the back of my hand, which hurt like hell and brought tears to my eyes. 'Ow, dammit!'

'Oh God, I'm sorry, that was my fault. Here.' Guy handed me a handkerchief that he'd pulled out of his pocket. 'Sorry, I didn't mean to make you jump. Are you OK?' He looked genuinely worried. Kyle was with him, and he simply looked embarrassed.

'I'm fine, honestly.' I dried my hand and wiped the mug before handing back the coffee-stained handkerchief.

'Guy, you idiot!' Lucy didn't look best pleased as she reached for the mug. 'Let me top you up, Sophie.'

'No, it's fine, honestly, I didn't lose much.' Looking up to see Kathy glaring at Guy, I sensed a little tension. 'You must have lots to do, we should get back to work.'

'Not really.' Guy put his hands in his pockets. 'We did most of it yesterday and Ben was planning on getting here early to finish off. He'll be in there now.' He nodded towards the Airstream. 'He's more of an early bird than us.' Turning towards Kathy's retreating back, he bellowed, 'Morning, Kathy.' There was no response, but she'd have had to have been deaf not to hear him. She'd made no effort to come and talk to us once he'd arrived, and now she was ignoring his greeting, which seemed out of character for the friendly woman I'd been introduced to yesterday.

The Airstream was still closed up. Ben hadn't opened the serving hatch or put out any signage, so it looked like an enormous silver bullet: very cool, but a bit soulless. I watched as Robin headed towards the back door, brandishing a handful of bin bags.

Lucy turned back towards the campervan. 'Well, I must get on. Thanks for stopping by, Sophie, and yes, it would be great to meet up. Just let me know when you're free.'

'I guess we should give Ben a hand.' I was surprised to hear Kyle's voice; he had been so quiet. 'Guy, are you coming?'

'Of course. Sorry again, Sophie. I definitely owe you a coffee now, so drop by when you're ready for your next top-up.' He smiled and turned, but had barely taken a step before the back door to the Airstream was flung open and Robin burst out.

'HELP, SOMEONE, HELP,' he cried. 'HE'S DEAD!'

CHAPTER 5

'*I* thought you were working on the theft at Berwick Hall.'

Joe sat next to me on a bench that had a great view of the Airstream. 'I am, I'm multi-tasking, and we're not exactly flush with officers right now.'

I still had hold of my Signal Box Coffee mug and turned it slowly in my hands. 'So how bad is it?'

'Pretty bad,' he replied. 'Poor guy had his head bashed in. It looks like whoever did it used one of those coffee things. You know – you bang it really hard, and then put coffee grounds in it before slotting it into the machine.' He mimed the actions of a barista.

'You mean the portafilter?'

He shrugged and gave me a blank look. 'If you say so. Anyway, one of those. It was lying on the floor covered in… well, you don't need to know, but there's a bloody great hole in his head.'

'Poor Ben. That's a horrible way to go. Is there any sign of a struggle?'

Joe nodded. 'Some, and it looks like a few things might have been taken. I'll need Guy or Kyle to confirm.'

Guy was talking to a uniformed police officer; Kyle was pacing up and down, seemingly in a different world. I nudged Joe and pointed in Kyle's direction.

'He looks like he's in shock, is there someone who can take care of him?'

'I'll make sure he's looked after. Now, you sure you didn't see anything unusual, anyone around the van?'

'You mean the Airstream? No, only Robin Scrimshaw. He was going round to every stall and handing out bin bags. We were all just chatting; Guy and Kyle thought Ben was in there working.'

Joe stood up and adjusted his belt. 'I'll send someone over to take a statement from you later.'

Before he had a chance to walk away, I had a question for him. 'Look, you're going to get this a lot, but when are the stalls around here going to be allowed to reopen?' Joe had told me not long after he'd arrived that the Food Festival was going to have to be closed, and now the area was buzzing with forensic officers in white suits, a number of them going in and out of the Airstream while police officers were carrying out interviews.

He was about to answer, but paused and looked intently at me. 'Are you concerned about the festival, the stallholders and the enjoyment of the visitors, or are you just wondering when you can get your hands on another coffee?' His eyes glanced down towards the mug in my hands, but when he looked back up at me, he was smiling. 'I know you have a severe addiction, but that's taking it a bit far.'

'It wasn't what I was thinking. I was just pre-empting the question you are going to start getting bombarded with, but now you mention it...' I looked over towards the red campervan. Lucy and Kathy were sitting silently outside, waiting their turn to be interviewed, and any desire to lighten the mood vanished. 'This is a pretty small community. Most of the stallholders know each other – they often end up at the same events, so this will hit a lot of people quite hard.'

I felt Joe's hand on my shoulder. 'I know. We'll get them back up and running as quickly as possible. I would imagine being able to get back to work will make it easier for them. There'll be a point when we can move the Airstream, which will make it all more bearable. Now, don't you have some cafés to run?'

'They're all really quiet during the festival; everyone comes out here to eat, so my team are probably twiddling their fingers.'

'Not all of them.' Joe nodded towards a couple of my Library team who were standing off to one side, watching the drama. They were probably on their break, but still, it wasn't very professional, especially as their uniforms were on display.

'Bloody hell!' I stood up, annoyed. 'I'll have a word. A bit of common sense wouldn't go amiss.'

'Go for it, dragon lady, speak later.' Joe walked off, pulling a notebook out of his back pocket. I marched off in the opposite direction to have a word with my team members. After metaphorically giving them a clip around the ear, I sent them back to work. With the festival closed, there was a good chance that visitors would make their way to the cafés.

Mark had already returned to the house to deliver a tour, but I didn't feel like following him yet. It seemed important to me to hang around; I was certain it wasn't some sort of gratuitous rubbernecking, which would have been a bad case of hypocrisy after sending my team members away for doing just that, but I'd been here when the body had been found, with the people who'd had the closest connection to Ben, and I felt the need to stay nearby. I was also, if I was honest, interested in finding out more.

I watched Kyle. He still looked slightly dazed, but at least he was holding a mug of something warm and hopefully sugary. He walked away from the police officer who had been questioning him, ducked under a strip of crime scene tape and sat down on the bench I'd just left. I returned and sat next to him.

'I'm so sorry.' I didn't know what else to say.

'Thanks. I can't believe it.'

'Had he worked for you for long?'

Kyle nodded. 'Couple of years. I'd gone to school with him not far from here – we're both local. We hadn't seen each other for years, then I went into business with Guy and we set up the office here in Derbyshire. Guy lives in London, but is on the road a lot so it didn't matter to him where the office was. I wanted to be near my family.' Kyle paused for a moment, his head hanging down. He hadn't looked at me since we'd started talking. 'I ran into Ben in a pub. He was looking for work and we needed an extra set of hands at events like this, so he came on board. He was great, a real hard worker. Pretty quiet, but he knew how to make a great cup of coffee.' He sat back on the bench and sighed. For the first time, I noticed that there were tears in his eyes. 'He was so excited about coming here – he loved Charleton, told us how his parents used to bring him here as a kid every summer.'

'He sounds like a nice guy.'

'He was.'

'So who would want to hurt him? Do you know if he'd crossed someone?'

Kyle shook his head. 'No, I really don't. I know he'd got himself into debt a couple of years ago, but that was all cleared up, or at least I thought it was. He...' Kyle shrugged and fell silent. I felt like I'd pushed him as far as I could.

'Kyle?' It was Joe, walking towards us. 'I'm sorry, but I'm going to need you down at the station. Routine, nothing to worry about.'

Kyle rose from his seat and turned towards me. He attempted to smile, but there were still tears in his eyes. Joe touched his arm gently and directed him towards a car that was waiting on the nearest gravel path.

As I stood up, I saw the next item on my agenda heading my way. Bruce from the Northern Bean Company was striding across the grass. Of course, when we'd agreed to reschedule our meeting to this morning, we'd had no idea that coffee would be the last thing on our minds.

The Northern Bean Company was a medium-sized business based in Manchester, our nearest large city, supplying numerous cafés and restaurants in the area. It was big enough to keep its prices lower than companies like Signal Box or Silver Bullet, but small enough that customers could feel pleased with themselves for not using the big international coffee roasters. The Northern Bean coffee was OK, but not particularly special. In my experience, it was quite dark and had a sort of smoky carbon flavour, so it was hard to taste the origins of the bean. It wasn't awful, just a bit on the predictable, commercial side for me.

'Hi, Bruce, I was just about to come looking for you. The police are closing off the gardens, so I'll walk you back towards the car park.'

'OK, fine,' he replied, looking rattled and sweaty.

'Are you OK?'

He nodded and pulled a bottle of water out of a pocket in his baggy cargo shorts. 'What a horrendous start to the day. I was meant to meet Ben yesterday. Poor guy. I just don't know what to say.' Bruce was glancing around as he spoke, looking as if his eyes weren't taking in anything that he saw. After a few moments' silence, he finally looked at me. 'Sorry I couldn't see you yesterday, something came up. I just wanted to check in with you. We have a new line of beans that you might be interested in, but now doesn't seem like the time to discuss it.'

It wasn't, and it certainly wasn't the time to tell him I was planning on finding someone else to supply our coffee beans.

Bruce was tugging at his shaggy beard as he spoke. With that and his shorts, he looked like the climbers on boulders and rock faces in the Peak District, practising their skills before heading off to climb mountains in Scotland or further afield in the Alps, maybe even fulfilling a dream of making it up Mount Everest.

All of a sudden, he seemed to pull himself together. 'Look,

Sophie, Charleton is a really important contract for us. I'll send you a couple of bags of the new stuff gratis and I'll do you a decent discount on your first order.' He sounded pretty confident that I'd like it, but I didn't have high hopes. I just nodded and politely thanked him. I hadn't been at Charleton House long before I'd learnt that Bruce was all about the sale; I don't think I'd ever had a conversation with him about the origins of his beans or what the company was doing to support the farmers, let alone what flavours he was passionate about or why he had got into the coffee business. It didn't look as if I was about to today, either.

'Any idea what happened?' It took me a minute to realise he had switched the conversation to Ben.

'No, none.'

We'd reached the path that would lead him to the car park. There were a couple of police officers standing guard, making sure no one came back into the gardens.

'Right, well, I'd better be off.' He stared back across the gardens to the stalls and the police activity around them before finally looking at me and shaking my hand. 'I'll have someone deliver those bags to you.'

With that, he was gone, his long strides powering him across the grass. He looked as if he was in a rush, but I wasn't at all sorry that our meeting had been shorter than usual.

I dismissed Bruce from my mind and set off towards the house. There were plenty of far more important and productive things I needed to do with my time. My feet crunched up the wide gravel path and I caught a glimpse of Mark in one of the windows, pointing out towards the gardens and probably explaining the history of the estate to a group of Russian businessmen. They'd asked for somewhere to land their helicopter, to borrow one of the Duke's private rooms to smoke cigars and drink champagne, and that none of the public go anywhere near them. What they'd got was the address of a football club ten miles away that might be prepared for them to land on the pitch, a tour with Mark in the same parts of the house as the general public, and extra members of our security team keeping an eye on them just in case they got difficult. The Duke and Duchess were happy to accommodate all sorts of requests, so long as they were reasonable and not the by-product of arrogance and wads of laundered cash.

I stopped to run my hand through a row of lavender plants that filled a long bed along the side of the path, and then brought it up to my nose, taking a deep breath. I'd picked up this habit from my father when I was a child and now I couldn't walk past a lavender plant without trailing my hand through it.

'*Lavandula angustifolia*, or common lavender.' Malcolm walked over to join me. 'Not a huge fan myself, reminds me of old aunts and grandmothers, but I once dated a girl whose family ran an enormous lavender farm in Provence so I know a bit about it. Beautiful – both the fields of lavender and the girl.' He was wearing, appropriately enough, a lavender coloured t-shirt tucked into cream cargo shorts and straining over his stomach. He was as ruddy faced as he had been at the drinks reception; even more so, if that was possible.

'Thought it was time I got out and about, got a bit of fresh air. Alex and I finished off a bottle of port last night. Well, I finished it off and he kept me company. Quite a night, eh?' He seemed to have no clue that the morning had been infinitely more eventful. I didn't have the energy to break it to him, and he'd find out soon enough if he tried to get into the gardens, so I played along.

'How was the Duke? Was he very upset?'

'Stoic, I guess you'd say. He talked a lot about the ceramicist. It was all rather dull; it's never been my kind of thing, but I guess it was part of my role as supportive friend to listen to him.' Malcolm didn't seem too concerned about any of it, but if he hadn't been in the Duke's life for a while, then maybe some of the emotional connection between the two men had waned.

'Were you very close when you were at university?'

Malcolm thought about the question for a moment. 'I suppose we were, not that we discussed that kind of thing. We left that for the girls. I was a little surprised, to be honest with you; I didn't think I had enough money to be accepted by his crowd as I had a very different upbringing. Normal, you'd probably call it. Father was the manager of a small local bank, mother stayed at home and looked after the children. It was the talk of the town when I got into Oxford. Of course, that was expected for Alex. Grandfather went, father went, Alex was next in line.

'There was a group of us who always dined together. Lots of champagne flowed and late nights drinking extortionately priced whisky. Of course, none of them had to worry about money. They spent summers in French châteaux, enjoyed endless skiing trips, that sort of thing. They were good enough to invite me on a couple of their jaunts and pay my way – very generous, but it certainly stung a bit, I can tell you. Sense of pride and all that.' He laughed, although it sounded more like a snort. 'They probably viewed it as a charitable act. Made me work damned hard, though. I was determined I'd be able to pay my own way once we graduated, show them I could match them pound for pound.'

He stopped and stared off into the distance. After what felt like a few awkward minutes, but was probably only seconds, he turned to look at me and smiled, and with a much more upbeat tone brought the subject to a close.

'Well, it seems to have worked. I've done pretty well for myself and the Duke remains a very generous man. I'm off for a stroll; it's too nice a day to be inside. Hope to run into you again later, Sally.'

I was about to correct him, but he had already set off.

I had expected the Library Café to be quiet, but not this quiet. However, I couldn't imagine it staying this way for long, unless the visitors assumed that the entire house was closed too. Tina was sitting at a table in the far corner, catching up on paperwork, a cappuccino and chocolate cookie beside her. A young member of staff stood behind the till, looking bored until she saw it was me who had walked in, at which point she jumped like someone had poked her from behind with something sharp.

'Sophie, is it true?' She started talking nineteen to the dozen. 'We saw all the police cars and someone said something about a dead body in the Great Pond, but I'm not due on a break yet so I've not been able to go and find out. Were you there?'

Tina joined us and tried to calm the girl down. 'Breathe, Chelsea, breathe. Let the poor woman sit down, I'm sure she'll tell us what she can in a moment.'

Tina had always been a steady, calming influence on the staff, and I often reminded myself how lucky I was to have her. When I'd arrived at Charleton House, she'd made my transition into a new job so much easier by keeping things running smoothly while I'd spent my time in endless meetings and learning the ropes.

I sank into one of the armchairs, the cold leather against my skin a relief after the intense heat out in the gardens.

'So, what's the gossip?' Tina was as keen as anyone to hear what had been going on.

'The body wasn't in the lake, it was in the back of that coffee Airstream. One of their staff. He'd been hit over the back of the head.'

'Was it a break in?'

'Joe said there were signs of a disturbance and things were missing, so that would make sense.'

I looked around the room. Only one table was taken and I recognised the customer as the Charleton House Health and Safety Manager. In a stiff grey suit, Anthony Leggett looked every inch a rule-making bureaucratic robot, but having sat in countless meetings with him, I knew that his exterior concealed a wicked sense of humour and someone with a firm grasp on the realities of working with the public.

'You can't account for the stupidity of people,' was one of his most often-used comments.

'Has it been this quiet all morning?' I asked Tina.

'Don't worry, it's not as bad as it looks. We had a mid-morning rush, three muffins and a packet of nuts. You'll be able to give us all pay rises.' She grinned. 'Really, don't worry, this happens every year. No one expects the cafés to make any money when the festival is on. Well, maybe a little in the Garden Café. Some of our older regulars still like to go in there for their afternoon tea, and dog walkers stop by the Stables Café.' Visitors didn't need a ticket to the house to reach the Stables Café, which took up a small space in an attractive cobbled courtyard within the eighteenth-century stable block, so it was hugely popular with cyclists, hikers and others exploring the 40,000 acre estate.

'Here in the Library,' Tina continued, 'we'll only see the staff who are too busy to go into the garden, which as it's a weekend is down to three people in IT with deadlines to meet and Anthony who's here to check everything's OK at the Food Festival. Mind you, that might change now. I'll make some extra sandwiches.'

I looked over at Anthony; he had his phone wedged between his shoulder and ear and was frantically making notes. I wondered if he'd expected to spend the day getting free food, when instead he'd got a dead body and a mountain of paperwork.

Tina looked up. 'Hang on, we're saved, the rush has arrived. We're about to sell at least one blueberry muffin, I'll go and book a cruise.'

I turned round to be greeted by a stony-faced Mark.

'Are you alright?'

'This is the face of a man who has spent the last ninety minutes talking into the wind.' He dropped into the armchair next to me. 'I love my job, I love telling the stories of this amazing house, and often I have to do that to people who aren't as interested in it as I am. You know, schoolkids who would rather be chasing the ducks on the Great Pond, journalists who are here because nothing has happened and their editor has forced them to go and do a piece on local tourist hot spots, or corporate guests who are only interested in the free alcohol. But this lot took the biscuit. They spent their time pointing at things and laughing, presumably claiming they have "three of these at home", ogling female visitors in shorts and checking their phones.'

'You mean the Russian group?'

'I do. But on the upside, a couple of little old ladies from Newcastle who attached themselves to the back of the group got a top quality tour for free, and the Russians' interpreter, who, to be fair, was hugely apologetic, gave me two hundred quid as a tip.'

'Bloody hell!' Chelsea shouted out. 'Maybe I should become a tour guide.'

Mark rolled his eyes at me and shouted back, 'Don't get too excited, I can't keep it. I'll take it down to the ticket office and get it recorded and put in the till.'

Chelsea looked disappointed and started straightening packets of nuts. Mark waited until she looked preoccupied by her own thoughts, and then focused on me again.

'So, any more developments? Does Joe have any leads?' As he talked, he removed his tie and rolled up his sleeves.

'No. I think he reckons a robbery, but he didn't say much. Far too early, I guess.'

'Well, he's supposed to be coming round for dinner tonight, so I'll see what I can get out of him. Bill has promised to make his favourite Eton Mess for dessert, but I might threaten to withhold it if he doesn't tell us what he's got so far. Do you want to come? There'll be plenty of food, and I could swear our friendly local bobby gets a twinkle in his eye every time he sees you.'

'Don't be ridiculous, Mark, there's no twinkling of any kind, nor will there be. We're friends, end of story.'

Mark pouted like a four-year-old. 'Spoilsport. Well, are you coming tonight?'

'Thanks, but no. I need a quiet night in after all this drama.' I dragged myself out of the chair. 'Promise me, no twinkle references over dinner. Don't go putting any ideas in Joe's head.'

'Like I said, spoilsport.' Mark stood up, spun dramatically and marched off towards the door. I knew I'd see him later; he could only go for a couple of hours before coming begging for free baked goods.

I liked to work in the Library Café kitchens, overlooking the back lane. Sometimes colleagues would stop for a chat through the window if they saw me there, and I felt like I had a reasonably good handle on life at the house as a result. Despite the festival being closed, not many visitors had made it to the Library Café yet, and Tina and her team were more than able to cope with those who had come in, so I'd decided to spend the afternoon trying out a couple of recipes.

I wasn't a trained pastry chef. I'd been employed at Charleton House to manage the cafés, and most of the cooking and baking was done by a husband-and-wife team Gregg and Ruth Danforth and the staff who worked for them, but I loved baking, and if I managed my time well, I was able to help out. Ruth was a great tutor and my skills were improving all the time, so I'd also been able to cut a few costs this way.

Right now, I was working on a very special project. Ruth had handed me the intimidating job of making the Duchess's birthday cake: an over-the-top super-indulgent chocolate creation. Ruth had been giving me hints and tips as I practised over the last couple of weeks, and I wanted to be able to present my final recipe to her on her return from holiday in a week's time.

I was measuring out ingredients when I spotted a familiar figure walking down the lane. It was the gardener who had almost knocked me to the ground and shouted at Ben yesterday afternoon, and he looked surprisingly tired for a guy with a healthy physique and muscles that popped out from under his t-shirt sleeves. I hadn't put two and two together before now, but an angry gardener and a dead body seemed, under the circumstances, to add up to a pretty reasonable four.

CHAPTER 6

I could feel four little feet pressing into the small of my back. I was cosy and had no desire to move, but the sun was streaming into my bedroom, and even with my eyes closed it was too much.

I rolled over, much to the frustration of Pumpkin, the enormous tabby cat who was under the sheets and pressing her feet against me like a toddler who had taken up half the bed and was after even more space. She let out an angry meow and repositioned herself, the end of her tail flicking back and forth. I was in trouble.

After climbing out of bed, I picked the book I'd been reading up from the floor, where it had fallen when I'd dozed off, rubbed the top of Pumpkin's head, pulled the sheets up over her and left her to it. She was most definitely in charge of the household, and I didn't want to disturb Her Majesty any more than was necessary. Especially on a Sunday, one of her seven days of rest.

I managed to make my way to the kitchen without falling down the stairs: a daily accomplishment which never fails to amaze me. Without my first coffee of the day, I doubt I could even tell anyone my name. On autopilot, I ground some beans in an antique cast-iron coffee grinder and set off the espresso maker. Pumpkin, who had deigned to venture down into the servants' quarters for breakfast, head-butted my leg as she passed by. I seemed to have been forgiven for the too-early wake-up call.

I sat at the kitchen table and stared at the logo on the side of the paper bag the coffee beans had come in: 'Signal Box Coffee'. My finished espresso was as good as the coffees Lucy had served me from the campervan, the quality was consistently high, and I knew I'd found my new favourite. Through bleary eyes, I registered the way the red of the Signal Box logo matched my red espresso maker and the enormous red fridge in the corner of the room. Everything about Lucy and Kathy's business suited me; it would be great to serve their coffee in the cafés.

I didn't know whether it was the espresso or the force of my idea, but I was wide awake. I wanted to start making changes in the cafés and this would be one of them: I was going to ask Signal Box Coffee to come on board and supply the coffee for Charleton House.

With that decision made, I found a spring in my step. I decided to forgo breakfast and made my way straight to the bathroom to get ready. Oh God, that was a mistake. The idea of looking in the mirror before I'd had my first coffee of the day had been a step too far, but not doing so before I put my glasses on was an unforgivable error. Most days, I thought that my spiky silver-grey hair looked cool; this morning, I just looked as if I had shoved my fingers in a plug socket. Well at least I didn't need to stress about roots showing or the cost of getting my hair dyed. This morning I might be capable of frightening small children, but it was all me and I loved it.

'Where's that scarf I gave you? I've told you before, you need brightening up. It's a beautiful summer's day and you look like you're off to a funeral.'

Joyce Brocklehurst was our brash retail manager and she wasn't one to beat around the bush. To be fair, she did have a point. After she had given me a bright colour-splotched scarf a couple of months ago, I had made a half-hearted attempt to look more like the creative café manager for an art-loving stately home, but it had soon petered out. My argument was that I rarely had time to go shopping and my wardrobe still reflected my previous life, managing restaurants and cafés in the business districts of London. Joyce's wardrobe, on the other hand, would probably require sunglasses and an active imagination. Today, her neck-breaking lime-green stilettos were paired with a peacock-blue pencil skirt that was so tight, I was amazed she could walk, and showed off her trademark 'visible panty line'. A purple silk shirt displaying an impressive cleavage finished the look.

Joyce had joined me in the Garden Café to see what gossip I could impart. After making us both a coffee, a smooth, creamy latte for Joyce and an espresso for myself, I walked behind her to a table, unable to take my eyes off her blonde bouffant hair which, combined with her heels, must have added almost a foot to her height. Every time I saw her, I wondered how she was able to walk around a house with cobbled courtyards, gravel pathways and uneven flagstones and not break an ankle every time she left one of the shops.

As we made our way through the café, more than a few eyes turned to take her in. Peacocks are not an uncommon sight in the stately homes of England, and it seemed Joyce was trying to ensure that Charleton House wasn't left out. We tucked ourselves away in a corner and she focused on me with her piercing blue eyes.

'So tell me, is it true that the body you found belonged to the young man who worked in that silver coffee van?' She peered at me over the china cup, her little finger raised in the air.

'It wasn't me who found him. Poor Robin from gardens was the one who stumbled across him, but yes, it was Ben.'

Joyce nodded. 'Ben Hines. I remember him running around in his football kit, muddy knees n'all. Always very polite.' That information surprised me, but then I knew he was local, so it shouldn't have been an enormous stretch that someone at Charleton would have known him. 'He went to school with my youngest daughter. I vaguely recall she had a crush on him, he was a nice lad. Such a shame.'

'If he was such a nice lad, how come he's ended up dead? Surely not everyone could have liked him.'

Joyce took her time placing the cup on the saucer, deep in thought.

'I've been wondering that since I heard. He must have been twenty-nine by now, so we're talking thirteen years since he was at school. I did hear that he'd got himself into a bit of trouble a while back...'

'Debt?' I interrupted, thinking back to what Kyle had said.

'Yes, that's it. We're not talking huge amounts of money, but enough for people to be unhappy with him. That was a while ago, though.'

'Do you think someone came back to collect and killed him when he didn't pay up?'

She looked at me intently for a moment or two. 'Sophie, dear, this is Derbyshire. The days of sheep rustling are long gone, and the Mafia have never, as far as I'm aware, taken control of any criminal underworld in the valleys. At worst, he'd have received a thumping round the back of the pub; at best, a cold shoulder or two. No, he was small time, and as far as I know, he'd sorted himself out.'

'But it's such an odd location for a random theft, we're in the middle of a country estate. It's not like someone could just happen to be passing and see an opportunity.'

'Think of all the dog walkers, hikers, tourists, locals out for a drive. There are no gates on the roads that run through here; locals use them to take short cuts on their commutes. That wouldn't explain how they got into the grounds of the house, I admit, but almost anyone could be in the general area.'

That didn't ease my mind. If this was an opportunist murder by someone who just wanted to empty the till and run, then maybe Charleton wasn't as idyllic as I had always thought.

Joyce appeared to read my mind. 'Still, it's a darned sight safer than that London and you must have been used to all the crime after, what? Fifteen years living there? Muggings on every street corner; having to walk everywhere clinging to your handbag in case someone snatches it; drinks being spiked in pubs; no one giving up their seats to old ladies on the bus. It's no wonder you moved back north.'

I couldn't help but chuckle at the mention of old ladies, but resisted the urge to make a joke at Joyce's expense. I'd rather be mugged on a street corner than offend Joyce with an ill-judged quip about her age.

'It's really not that bad. Anyway, Charleton looks far more dubious this morning. Police still crawling all over the garden; photographers trying to get past security to find a vantage point in the house where they can take pictures of where it happened.'

'Ah, but these are special circumstances. It happens all the time in London.'

'You're spending too much time reading scare stories on the internet. I loved London; I was just ready to come home.'

'Well, I'm a born-and-bred Derbyshire lass,' Joyce replied with pride, slipping back into the northern accent that she was, ironically and unsuccessfully, forever trying to tame, especially around the Duke and Duchess. 'I've never left and I never will. There isn't anythin' you can get in London that you can't get up 'ere, whether it's style, food or culture, and all in a much better setting.'

In many ways I couldn't argue with her, and when it came to

style, she certainly didn't have any competition. Mainly because she'd scared it all off.

'You can lead a quiet life round here if you want, Sophie, although you're still a bit too young for the pipe and slippers routine. Whatever you returned north looking for, it was a good move. Joe will figure out who killed poor Ben and we can all go back to smelling the roses, or your baking, without having to worry about a killer being on the loose, which is a permanent possibility in London.'

'Was that meant to be comforting, Joyce? The words "killer on the loose" aren't going to help me sleep tonight.'

'Don't be soft, girl. Knock back a glass of something strong before you go to sleep, then when you wake, put on your brightest, sunniest outfit. Works for me when I've got something on my mind.' I looked at her lime-green fingernails and her matching earrings – solid discs at least an inch wide that swung with every movement. Now I was keen to see her choice of outfit on a day she was feeling depressed. That thought alone perked me up and I smiled at her, grateful that this slightly bonkers, slightly scary, but wonderful rainbow of a woman had entered my life.

'That's more like it.' She beamed back at me. 'Now, another slice of cake each and all will be well in the world.'

CHAPTER 7

Within Charleton House are two outdoor courtyards. From above, the building looks like a square-cornered figure of eight. One of these courtyards is cobbled and dates back to the original Tudor building – it is said that Henry VIII dropped by during one of his processions north. On one wall is a stone archway, housing a heavy wooden door, low enough to cause taller visitors to duck their heads as they make their way into the room beyond. Previously a wine cellar, on normal days it is full of replica wine barrels.

Today, however, the space had been transformed into a seventeenth-century coffeehouse to complement the Food Festival, the wine theme having already been brought to life the previous year. The windows had been covered up and faux candles flickered along the windowsills. A small amount of 'smoke' hovered in the air and a long table dominated the room. Visitors of all ages sat around the table, and others stood around the walls awaiting the eleven o'clock performance. With my own coffee obsession, there had been no way I was going to miss this. I was keen to learn more about the bean that kept me functioning and pleasant to be around.

The chatter of the crowd hushed as a tall man ducked under the doorway and made his way into the room. He was a startling figure in a low-crowned beaver-fur hat trimmed with ribbons and feathers. Below that he wore a wig, which must have been unbearably hot in the August heat. As he came down the stairs, I got a good look at the rest of him. He was wearing a suit of biscuit brown wool: a long straight-cut knee-length coat with elbow-length sleeves over a waistcoat almost as long. His full-sleeved shirt was worn with a cravat tied in a knot at his throat. Breeches that finished just below the knee over stockings and square-toed shoes tied at the instep with ribbons finished the look, and his entire outfit was dotted with knots of brown and beige silk. In one hand, he carried a pair of gloves; his other rested on the hilt of a sword that hung from his waist.

He scanned the room, a smile forming on his lips. 'How wonderful to see so many enquiring minds, seeking knowledge and good conversation over that most virtuous of drinks, coffee. I see some familiar faces, but for those of you who don't know me, I am Samuel Pepys, diarist and politician. I have of course filled my life with other noble professions, but I won't bore you with that for now, for we are here in the year of Our Lord 1676, in this simple yet welcoming coffeehouse, to debate matters of the day, learn of mathematics and science. If we feel the need for something a little more light hearted, we can take bets on a bear fight. You can even get a haircut – not something I'll be doing, of course.'

He smiled and winked as he tossed some of the long hair of his wig over his shoulder.

'You see, ladies and gentleman,' – he paused – 'although I am surprised to see ladies in here. Normally the fairer sex never frequent a coffeehouse; it's really not the place for you respectable ladies. Do you know' – he spoke quietly, sharing his surprise with the crowd – 'there are some women who would like to see coffeehouses closed down, saying that their menfolk are wasting their time here, that coffee weakens us, turns us into babbling fools and makes us unable to... well, erm, fulfil our, shall we say, manly duties.'

He slowly circled the table, stopping from time to time to make a point or single out a visitor, looking them in the eyes and bringing them into his confidence.

'I find coffee a marvellous stimulant, and it contains, so I am told, many medicinal qualities. It will cure you of gout and scurvy. Children in particular can be found in much better health after consuming it. However, I don't recommend drinking it after dinner, unless you wish to avoid sleep for some hours. But it's not just the coffee that brings me here to this "penny university", for that is what the coffeehouses are sometimes called. I assume you all paid your penny at the door in order to enter? And once you're here, the learning available to you makes them worthy of that name. Literature, politics, science – just sit down next to a stranger and discuss any subject that takes your fancy. Revolutions have been planned, scientific experiments carried out. It is said that one Isaac Newton dissected a dolphin on a table in a coffeehouse that goes by the name of Grecian.'

He was pointing at the table, indicating the length of the dolphin and getting the visitors to picture the scene.

'My personal favourite is Will's near Covent Garden. It is a particularly literary crowd that you'll find in attendance and it is there that you will find me enjoying a dish of coffee. I'm not short of choice, however, as we are well on our way to having over a thousand coffeehouses in London alone.'

As Samuel Pepys talked to the crowd, a few visitors quietly came and went through the door in the corner. One of them caught my eye: Kathy from Signal Box Coffee, the quieter of the two sisters. She looked tired and distracted. Tucked away in the shadows, she watched the performance with glassy eyes, but didn't really seem to be taking it in. She just stared in the general direction of Pepys.

As I returned my attention to the action, I spotted another familiar face enter the room: Guy Glover. This was turning into some sort of coffee roasters' reunion. He scanned the room, paying no attention to Pepys and his performance. Spotting Kathy, he made his way over to her, stood by her side and whispered into her ear. She jumped and turned, realising who it was. Her face taking on an expression of fury, she immediately turned and left. With a look of amusement, Guy shook his head and casually leant against the wall, clearly in no rush to follow her.

I turned back to hear Samuel Pepys asking a visitor if he could have his seat as his feet were weary. Then, loud enough for everyone to hear, he directed his comments at those around the table. He was telling them all of King Charles II's 1675 proclamation, which attempted to suppress coffeehouses.

'You see, my friends, his fear was that political debate, which had previously only been the activity of the elite, was now being encouraged among the middle classes, and that coffeehouses were hotbeds of revolutionary talk and possible violence against authority, including the Crown. He lost that battle. I have a feeling that coffeehouses will be here for a very long time to come. Now if you'll excuse me, I need to fetch my wife. I would never allow her to join me in a coffeehouse and she has the good sense not to ask. It has been a pleasure speaking with you all.'

With that, he swept out of the door and disappeared. The visitors applauded and gradually left the room until only a few remained to read through the replica seventeenth-century newspapers and pamphlets that were scattered on the table.

Guy had already gone.

Inspired by my encounter with Samuel Pepys, I felt the need for another coffee. Making myself a latte, very different from the gritty, overly sweetened jet-black sludge that Pepys himself would have found pleasure in, I took the mug into my office, hidden behind a door at the back of the Library Café kitchen.

I immediately regretted it. One of the quirks of working in a building like Charleton House is the varying degrees of temperature you experience throughout the year. In the winter, my office is cold enough to freeze ice cubes; in the summer, when I could do with those ice cubes, I feel like I'm sitting in one of my ovens. At least my matchbox-sized office is homely and close to some of my team. I have colleagues who are in attic spaces and can't stand up straight. One shares a corridor with a photocopier and another is convinced his room is haunted by the ghost of an old housekeeper. He never works beyond six o'clock at night, when he swears she comes in and tries to share the desk with him.

Right now, however, I felt no sympathy for any of them as a bead of sweat ran down my forehead, and I'd only been in my office long enough to turn on my computer.

'Sophie, have you got a minute?' Chelsea called from the end of the kitchen. With no regret, I abandoned my office, went out to the café and found myself face to face with Kathy.

'I'm really sorry to bother you, but I was wondering if you had heard anything about when, or if, the festival will be reopening. It's just, I saw you with that detective, and no one else is telling us anything. Lucy thought it was worth seeing if you knew anything – maybe there has been a staff memo?'

'No, I'd be the last to know. I'm sure the police will hand the gardens back over to us as soon as they can.'

'I guess so. We saw the Airstream being taken away on a trailer, so maybe it won't be too long. Sorry to disturb you, we're just frustrated. This weekend was a big opportunity for us.'

She looked more than just frustrated; she was pale and distracted.

'Is everything OK? You look a bit under the weather; can I get you a drink or something to eat?'

She shook her head. 'I'm just tired, and this has all been a bit of a shock.'

'Did you know Ben well?'

'In a way. We often ended up at the same events. I can't believe what's happened. He was one of those gentle giants, built like a rugby player, but really sweet and kind. We always helped each other out if we ran out of anything. He gave us a hand when we ran out of petrol once and couldn't get off site at a concert.'

I decided to chance my arm. 'What about Guy? Did he work with Ben a lot or was he mainly in the background of the operation?'

At the mention of Guy's name, she met my eyes and froze, then glanced away.

'I better go. I've left Lucy on her own.' With that, she was off and out of the door, and I was left staring after her, a little surprised at how quickly she'd managed to scurry away. Something was going on between her and Guy, and as much as it was none of my business, I was curious to know more.

'No gin? Really? Are you sure you're feeling alright?'

Mark and I had decided to end the day at the Black Swan, a beautiful English country pub that would look at home on the front of a postcard. It was our nearest pub in the pretty village of Hadshaw, just within the boundary of the Charleton House estate, and was another property owned by the Fitzwilliam-Scott family. It was everything that an English pub should be and we were lucky to be able to call it our local. I was doubly lucky to live only a couple of doors away, so getting home safely was never a problem. Not that I often over indulge; I value my early mornings far too much.

Mark and I had found a table to sit at out in the garden. It was a warm evening, and to my mind it was worthy of a glass of Pimm's. As has become the tradition, I only ever indulge in this quintessentially English gin-based liqueur when the sun draws me outside without the need for a sweater. Combined with lemonade, the glass filled with chopped cucumber, oranges, lemons and strawberries, and a few mint leaves, the drink screams 'English summer'.

'There's gin in it, so near enough,' I responded.

'But I enjoy picking one out for you, finding the most ridiculous name.' Mark knew I was attempting to try every one of the seventy gins that the Black Swan served. 'You're ruining my evening.' He moved off towards the door, ducking to avoid the roses that were hanging low off the trellis that surrounded it.

I closed my eyes...

'You're snoring.'

I woke with a start as Mark put the glasses on the table. 'What?'

'You were snoring. The poor family at the next table had to move, it was so bad.' He gestured to the family two tables over, making sure he spoke loudly enough for them to hear.

'I was not.'

I turned to see the family all trying to stifle laughs, looking back and forth between them and Mark a couple of times.

Mark eventually smirked. 'You are so easy, of course you weren't.'

I smiled sheepishly at the family, and then turned back to Mark, stealing the bag of crisps he had brought out with him as punishment. We enjoyed an easy silence as we savoured the first few mouthfuls of our drinks.

Mark was the first to break the peace. 'Do you think the two thefts are related? Berwick Hall and here at the house? It's too much of a coincidence.'

'True, but they're very different. Berwick Hall was during the day when visitors were around. Or at least, Joe got the call during visitor hours, so I assume that's what happened. The St Ives bowl was taken during a private evening event, so only specific people were allowed onsite. It would have been a mighty coincidence for someone working the event to have also been a visitor at Berwick.'

'True.' Mark thought for a little while. 'And the body?'

'Joe's first thoughts were a robbery. Ben did owe some people money, but only small amounts and he seemed to be well liked.'

Mark took a big gulp of beer. 'Maybe we're dealing with an over-caffeinated rivalry.' His voice was dripping in comic conspiracy. 'The Signal Box women are tired of being in the shadow of the big shiny Airstream, their coffee sales are falling as their cute campervan just can't compete with the hypnotising gleam of the silver bullet. One of them snaps and suffocates Ben in a bag of beans. The autopsy is going to reveal hundreds of coffee beans in his ears, up his nose and down the back of his throat. The only clue will be that a single bean among all those found on him will come from the Signal Box.' He looked at me through half open eyes, as though assessing a potential suspect.

'Did you enjoy that?' I asked. He had certainly seemed to get a lot of pleasure out of his little fantasy. He shrugged and returned to his normal voice.

'It's a thought, I'll run it past our resident detective in the morning. He'll be forever in my debt for solving the crime.'

I loved Mark, but he could be an idiot sometimes. 'Well the first problem you have is he was killed with a portafilter, not beans.'

'But that still means he was killed by coffee, sort of. I keep telling you that too much of that stuff isn't good for you.'

I spluttered as my laughter coincided with a mouthful of Pimm's, then moved him on to something more serious.

'Kathy wasn't happy today. Each time I saw her, she looked miserable and on edge. Something is certainly bothering her.'

'The one with the long hair? I didn't notice. I remember seeing her in here on Friday night, though. She must be staying here as she went up to the guestrooms.'

Not only was the Black Swan the sweetest English pub with a killer gin list, but it also had the most exquisitely designed guest rooms. The Duchess herself had led the interior design, and I'd experienced one of the rooms first hand when I'd come for my interview at Charleton House and needed somewhere to stay the night before. I hadn't wanted to leave the next morning, the room was so nice, but I figured trying to claim squatter's rights wouldn't have gone down too well with my new employers.

'But they're local, aren't they? I don't see why they'd book to stay here during the festival.' I instinctively looked around the garden, just in case either of the sisters was there and could hear us.

'It's not uncommon. Some just decide it's easier and like the idea of not having to cook for themselves, or they want to make a weekend of it and enjoy being on the estate the whole time. If there are celebrity guests who aren't important enough to stay with the Duke and Duchess, they'll be put up here.'

I thought about what Mark had just said. There was one easy way to find out, plus it was my turn to get the drinks in. I gathered up our empty glasses and made my way into the cool, dark pub. The low ceilings were covered in wooden beams and an enormous stone fireplace stood at the far end of the room, but it was too hot a day to appreciate the cosy atmosphere.

After choosing a glass of Crooked Spire Summer Gin and tonic, I watched the landlord hand pull Mark's pint of English porter.

'Such a shame, what happened up at the house.' The landlord had seen me often enough to recognise me. 'I hope the police catch who did it quickly, then we can all rest in our beds again.'

I nodded. 'Am I right in thinking that some of the stallholders are staying here?'

'You are. All five rooms are booked and all to people working the festival. Two of them to that poor lad's friends.'

'Ben's friends? Do you mean Guy and Kyle who worked with him?'

'That's them. He wasn't staying here, but they've both got rooms.'

'What about the other coffee company, run by two women?'

He shook his head. 'We've got a cheesemaker and his wife, and two chocolatiers, but no more coffee roasters. It's marvellous having them stay, mind. We've had some great conversations and I might end up doing business with the cheesemakers. There you are, love, enjoy.'

He handed me the two glasses and I walked back out to Mark with a spring in my step.

'What do you look so cheerful about?'

'The mystery continues.' I peered over the top of my glasses at him, attempting to look conspiratorial, but I probably just looked drunk. 'Kathy isn't staying here so she must have been visiting someone. The question is, who?'

'Well I remember that Ben followed almost immediately after her, but I just assumed he was staying here too.'

I took a long, cool drink. A honey blossom infused gin had sounded perfect for summer, but to be honest, it was a bit odd.

'Ben being here kind of makes sense. If his colleagues were staying here, then they might have been meeting to discuss business, or just having a relaxing drink in the quiet of one of their rooms after setting up for the festival. That seems reasonable enough, but why would Kathy be here? I didn't get the impression that the two coffee companies were particularly friendly.'

'What if...' Mark let the words hang in the air and attempted to wink. 'What if there was a bit of "how's ya father" going on?'

'Don't be daft, she was not sleeping with any of them.'

'Why not? They end up at events together, they get to know each other. The next thing is they're falling in love over a bag of coffee beans, very romantic.'

It didn't make sense to me. There hadn't been many signs of a professional relationship between the two companies, let alone simmering sexual desire.

'Kathy was always keeping to herself, not fluttering her eyelashes at the Silver Bullet crew.'

'What if that was intentional? What if she's sleeping with the enemy, so to speak, and is hiding it from her sister?' He paused for a moment, thinking it all through. 'She's hiding the relationship and comes over here for a sneaky fumble. Ben arrives at the pub at the same time to go and meet whichever one she isn't sleeping with and follows her upstairs. She sees Ben, or he later says something to her, and out of fear of all being revealed to her sister, she bashes him on the back of the head and her dirty little secret dies with him.'

Mark looked very pleased with himself. I wasn't sure how to respond so I sat back and drank some gin. Personally I felt the angry gardener was a stronger suspect, but sex had played a part in plenty of murders before, and as much as I didn't really know Kathy, she was definitely a woman with something on her mind.

'Are you planning on putting your deerstalker hat on?' Mark disturbed me from my thoughts.

'Am I what?'

'Sherlock Holmes's deerstalker hat. I can hear the cogs turning, I think you're trying to figure out who killed Ben.'

I couldn't deny I was more than a bit curious, and there were already two suspects. This was going to need another gin and tonic to oil the cogs.

CHAPTER 8

$\mathcal{A}$fter upsetting Pumpkin because I wouldn't lounge around in bed all day with her sprawled on my chest, her nose in my face, I made myself a quick espresso and then jumped in the car. I always enjoyed coming in to work, but today I was especially keen. The cogs had continued to turn as I lay in bed last night, but I had so little information to go on, I didn't get very far. I needed to know more.

I'd received a text from Joe in the early hours: the festival had received the all clear and could open again. The stallholders were never going to make up for their lost takings, but hopefully a combination of good weather, passionate foodies and, let's face it, macabre curiosity would lead to a decent number of visitors and the weekend wouldn't be a complete failure for them.

This morning I had decided to shower some love and attention on my Stables Café staff, also known as checking up on them and making sure everything had been kept to a high standard while I'd been distracted with events at the festival. This was the one café that would still have done a reasonable amount of trade while the festival was on, and that hadn't changed just because the garden had been closed, so the team hadn't been able to take it easy. The Stables Café was popular with people who wanted to spend time outdoors, and another hot day had been forecast so it was likely they would be busy.

The café shared a large cobbled courtyard with a gift shop and a number of horse-related exhibitions that reflected the Fitzwilliam-Scott family's love of the animal. The café team was doing a good job, so after a quick meeting with the supervisor, fending off dozens of questions about the murder from the team while helping them open up and serve the first few customers of the day, I was ready to leave them to it. I knew they would be distracted and eager for gossip, but under the circumstances there was little I could do to prevent that, so long as it didn't get out of hand.

'Excuse me, are you the manager?' Queries that started like this were rarely good news. 'I have a complaint to make.' As I turned and looked at the owner of the voice, I laughed. It was Joe.

'Oh, give me strength. I hope you're not expecting a coffee.' His mouth fell, forming a cartoon-like sad face. 'Walk with me to the Library Café and by the time we get there I might have changed my mind.'

We set off out of the courtyard, took a short cut through a sweet little walled garden and down the lane to the staff entrance into the house. I was enjoying the warmth of the sun on my face; as far as the weather went, the Food Festival had been lucky. I'd heard tales of thunderstorms in previous years, of flooded gardens and sausage rolls floating away, never to be seen again. Staff drove past us on golf buggies, and I felt a brief childlike stab of jealousy. I loved the idea of whizzing around the grounds on one of those, but I never had a reason to do so.

Joe woke me from my mental meanderings. 'Penny for your thoughts.'

'Hmm? Oh, nothing special. I've been thinking about the murder.'

'You and me both, and if you've any ideas, I'd love to hear them. Everyone is alibied up to the hilt.'

'Did you know Ben? You both grew up around here.'

'No, he's much younger than me, but thanks for the compliment. Plus he went to a different school to me where the kids tended to be from another area.'

We turned the corner into the Library Café, our eyes quickly adjusting to its shadows, the natural light being limited to a couple of tiny windows and the few rays that escaped from the kitchen every time someone opened the door. I pointed in the direction of a table tucked away in the corner.

'Go and grab a seat, and I'll fetch some coffees.'

'Already sorted,' Tina called out across the room, making her way towards me and smiling. 'I saw you coming down the lane when I was in the kitchen.'

I was impressed, although it suggested she also knew how to soften me up.

'Can I grab a moment with you and Joe?'

'Sure, come on.'

Tina pulled up a chair. 'It's nothing major, it's just that I was in The Old Oak pub last night and there was a young lad in there selling off some of the coffee from that van.'

'From Silver Bullet Coffee?' Joe sat up straight.

'Yeah, the silver van thing, where the guy was killed.'

The Old Oak was a pub in a small village about five miles from Charleton House. I'd been told it was nothing special – there was the occasional fight or drugs-related issue, but it was mainly the work of small-time local troublemakers and not particularly newsworthy.

'Did you recognise him?' Joe had pulled out a notepad and pen.

'No, but he seemed to know quite a few of the locals. No one wanted to bother with him.'

'That's great, Tina. I'll have a catch up with Sophie, then I'll arrange for you to make a formal statement. Thanks for letting me know.'

Tina stood as the drinks were brought to our table. 'Not a problem, you know where to find me.'

Once we were alone, Joe grinned at me. 'Well that helps my theft theory.'

'So you still think that's what happened? Ben was the victim of a robbery?'

'Maybe. I really don't have much to go on. Everyone else who was in the area has a pretty solid alibi.'

'Even the angry gardener?'

'What angry gardener?'

'Oh sorry, I thought Mark would have told you. He barged into me on Friday afternoon, shortly before confronting Ben, and he was seriously mad. I'm afraid he was too far away for us to hear what he was saying to Ben.'

'Ah, that angry gardener. Yes, Lucy told me he nearly sent you flying. He's called Elliot Forrester and he was working with Robin, his supervisor, when Ben was killed. Robin's a fan of spreadsheets, so he knows exactly what's being worked on when, where and who's doing it.'

'What about Kyle and Guy?'

He shook his head. 'All spoken for. Kyle was having breakfast at the Black Swan and was seen by the landlord, and Guy was meeting Malcolm De Witt up in his room.'

'The Duke's friend? What was Guy doing in his room? A secret assignation?' I couldn't imagine anything less likely, but people could surprise you.

'Ha! Hardly – what a thought. No, Guy was giving him advice on investing in restaurants. Apparently that's Guy's background and he sometimes works as a consultant. Malcolm is thinking of investing in a new restaurant in London.' I must have still looked a bit nonplussed, because Joe added, 'Malcolm has a separate sitting room to himself, they weren't having a meeting on the bed.'

I laughed. 'I was starting to picture that. What about Kathy from the Signal Box?'

Joe took another mouthful of coffee and put the mug down. 'What about her?'

I explained what Mark had seen and the theory that was knocking around my head.

'A crime of passion?' Joe looked thoughtful. 'That's a damn sight more interesting than a robbery, it would certainly liven things up. I'll double check her alibi and keep it in mind, but I don't think we're going to get a "made for TV" sex and murder special out of this. It'll be something much more mundane.'

'Mundane? A murder at Charleton House? You're kidding, right? You could be fishing bodies out of the Manchester Ship Canal, but instead you're in the glorious surroundings of one of the country's finest historic houses. Don't start taking it for granted.'

I peered at him over the top of my glasses, looking for signs of a twinkle I really didn't want to find. Bloody Mark, putting thoughts into my head. I needed a distraction so gathered up our empty mugs.

'Any word on the thefts, are they related?'

Joe was straightening his tie and tucking in his shirt. He always had a slight air of a dishevelled schoolboy.

'You need to stop asking me questions I can't answer.' He sighed dramatically. 'Well, one happened long enough after the other that they could have been done by the same person, but the Berwick theft was during public opening hours and was a miniature painting that could have been slipped into someone's bag. Charleton was a private event, and you would have had a hard time sneaking the bowl out unless you had a decent sized holdall to put it in. And everyone with a big bag was checked as they left, guests and staff.'

'So it was an inside job?'

'No, I'm not saying that, but I reckon it was planned. I'm sure that Berwick was the work of an opportunist who saw a chance and took it. Sadly they're both on the backburner now; the murder comes first and we haven't got the resources to focus on the robberies too. I'm still technically on the Berwick case and I'll do my best, but it's not a priority right now.' It looked as if his two days of dead ends were getting to him. 'But I've been really lucky. Most new detectives would be shuffling papers back at the station, checking statements, doing background checks, that sort of thing. DS Harnby only has me out and about because we're short of feet on the ground, and she knows that people are used to seeing me around here so are likely to open up. I need to come up with something useful, though, or she'll have me chained to a chair again.'

Concern was scored into the crease across his forehead. I went back to the counter and wrapped up a huge slice of lemon drizzle cake; I couldn't tell him who had murdered Ben, but I could give him a sugar rush and a reason to loosen his belt a notch!

I angled the bratwurst so the tomato sauce wouldn't drip onto my skirt, tilted my head back and took another enormous bite. This was no scrawny hotdog, but really good-quality meat from Derbyshire born-and-bred farm stock and I was already thinking about having a second.

Mark and I were sitting facing the Great Pond, soaking up the sun and watching a family of ducks swim in single file across the water. The gardens team had installed little ramps on either side of the pond's concrete base to make it easier for the ducks, who were clearly considered part of the family, to climb in and out. I watched the crowds of visitors as they shuffled from stall to stall, countless different languages and accents filling the air along with the sweet scents of freshly baked cookies and breads. A gentle breeze could change everything and the smells of sizzling bratwurst or melting cheese would take over. I shuffled along the bench a little; I seemed to be in prime position for getting my knees bashed by shopping bags as people passed by.

On the opposite side of the pond was a gap where the Airstream had been, and the immediate area remained closed off. A few visitors were milling around looking at the gap, no doubt speculating as to what had happened, but the majority weren't paying it any attention. For those not immediately involved, Ben's murder was quickly becoming yesterday's news, and that didn't feel right. I couldn't stop picturing the gentle-looking man who had seemed so dejected when Elliot Forrester had confronted him.

'There you are.'

I looked up for the source of the voice and found myself face to face with a wall of navy and white checked fabric that turned out to be a summer dress clinging to Joyce's various curves. She had adorned it with every fuchsia pink accessory you could think of: a wide belt with an enormous buckle; a cluster of bangles on each wrist; a chunky necklace that could be mistaken for a string of child's toy bricks. Fuchsia-pink sunglasses were balanced on the top of her head and a pair of fuchsia pink stilettos made me wonder how she didn't get vertigo. I also couldn't understand how she wasn't sinking into the grass, so I took a closer look and saw she had an ingenious plastic plug on each heel that stopped them acting like sharp blades.

'Brilliant!' I hadn't meant to say it out loud.

'What's that, dear?' Joyce followed my eye line. 'Oh yes, stops me looking like a drunk guest at a garden party. Also means I can come and find you two and not miss out on all the fun. Budge up.' She had a plastic flute of prosecco in her hand; she shouldn't have been drinking while at work, but I couldn't think of anyone brave enough to confront her. Settling herself next to me, she looked across the water at the gap in the stalls.

'So sad. I'm really struggling to picture someone wanting to kill the boy I remember at the school gates all those years ago.' She stared off into the distance, I assumed picturing Ben as a kid in his school uniform.

'Did you ever hear of him getting involved in anything? I know about the debt, but anything else? He seemed like such a nice, mild-mannered man, but he must have been involved in something.'

Joyce shook her head. 'Like I said, love, it's been years since I last saw him. I've certainly not heard of anything. Tom might know more.' She was looking across the crowds in the direction of the stall we'd got our bratwursts from. 'Tom Bidwell, the butcher. He was one of those Ben owed money to for a while. He might know more about what was going on with him. Tell him how much you liked your sausage and I'm sure he'll talk to you.'

'Will he give us a couple more of these?' asked Mark. I'd almost forgotten he was there. He took the last bite of his bratwurst, a large drip of mustard making a bid for freedom and landing on his tie.

I had a better idea. 'How about I get a serving of haggis, neeps and tatties for us all to share instead?'

I felt two sets of eyes swivel in my direction. 'I beg your pardon?' Joyce sounded horrified.

'Haggis, neeps and tatties. Haggis is traditionally served with mashed swede – neeps – and potatoes – tatties.'

'I know very well what it's served with. You could serve it with caviar and a jeroboam of Dom Pérignon and you'd still not get me anywhere near it. I'm stunned that you'd suggest I'd consume peasant food. You do know what it's made from?'

'I do, it's fantastic stuff. I'd choose it as my last meal if I found myself on death row.'

'Bring it anywhere near me and you might have that opportunity.'

'Ladies.' Mark had found the nerve to come between my love for haggis and Joyce's strong feelings. 'Don't worry, Joyce. Sophie is going to wait until we have both gone before she goes anywhere near that stall.'

'Of course she is,' agreed Joyce, 'she knows what's good for her.' She peered into the distance again, distracted by something. 'Bugger. Well I guess my break has come to a sudden end. Those two are meant to be looking after the courtyard gift shop while I'm in meetings.'

We followed her eye line to a couple of young women on the other side of the pond.

'What meetings?' Mark was clearly feeling brave.

'This meeting, Mark, this meeting. You can call it cross-departmental integration and development if you like, but whatever it is, it's over. I need to go and round up my errant staff.' She swallowed what was left of the prosecco in one gulp and handed the empty flute to Mark. 'Make sure you recycle it, we can save the planet one drink at a time.' Then she tottered off, slowly but with fierce determination.

Tom Bidwell was taking a break at the back of the stall, sitting on top of a wooden box, writing a message on his phone as I came round the corner.

'Tom?'

He didn't look up. 'Who wants to know?'

'Sophie, I'm a friend of Joyce's.'

'Who?'

'Joyce Brocklehurst, I work at the house with her.'

He stood up and looked at me for the first time. 'Any friend of Joyce is a friend of mine. Fine woman. How can I help you, Sophie?'

'It's about Ben, the man who...'

'Died, I know. Bloody awful. What about him?'

I was unsure about talking to a stranger about their financial affairs, but I got the impression that mentioning Joyce hadn't just unlocked a door for me, it had firmly wedged it open.

'Sorry for being quite so personal, but I believe that he used to owe you money.'

He stared at me. 'Joyce told you, I assume. Yes, he did. Why are you interested?'

I wasn't entirely sure how to answer that, so I decided to be honest. 'I don't know. I was there when his body was found and I can't stop thinking about it. I guess I need to make sense of it.'

'Isn't this in the hands of the police?'

'Yes, but... well, I'm here onsite. Maybe I'll find something that can help them.'

Tom laughed. 'I don't know what your job is, but it must leave you with a lot of spare time on your hands. Either that or you're management and have a talent for delegation.'

I couldn't help but laugh at that. He read my response perfectly.

'Management, eh? Well, I better not waste your time. Have a seat.' He removed a bag of bread rolls from the top of another box and gestured towards it. I sat down. 'I had a lot of time for Ben. He worked for me and was a real grafter. I had no problem lending him money when he asked a few years back; I trusted him, but not long after that, he just stopped coming into work. I'd see him cross the road to avoid me. If I did catch him, he always promised I'd get the money back and then made an excuse, so after a while I gave up. It was only a couple of hundred quid; it wasn't worth making a fuss.'

'When was this?'

Tom closed his eyes. 'Hmm, about three years ago. Yeah, three years ago. I remember because it was the year we had that awful summer and it didn't stop raining. A couple of times I ran into him and he was wearing sunglasses, which was ridiculous because we barely saw the sun that year. I eventually realised he was hiding one hell of a black eye.' He laughed at the memory. 'The daft sod, should have just claimed that the other guy looked a lot worse. Turned out he owed some bloke down the pub fifty quid and he was more worried about getting the cash back than I was.'

Tom didn't sound like a man who was bitter. In fact, he didn't seem to bear Ben any ill will at all.

'What happened to him after that? Did you hear any more about him?'

'Only that he was in and out of work, owed a few others money, and then I got wind of this coffee job and I started to see him at some of the food events in the area. Far as I know, he didn't pay off any of his debts, but he seemed to sort himself out. You know, he was always working, and he had that money he'd borrowed off folks and not repaid, yet he was always in the same jeans and rugby shirts, and drove an old car his mother had given him years ago. Still lived with her too. Most blokes his age would get themselves a flash car or fancy watch, but there was nothing like that. I don't know what he was doing with his money, but he wasn't spending it on himself, that's for sure. I can't tell you much else, I'm afraid. He was a good lad; I don't know what he got himself mixed up in, but I'm sure he didn't deserve this.'

I thanked Tom. It had been a brief but incredibly helpful conversation, and I was starting to build up a picture of Ben. Not a detailed one, but enough to give me a slight sense of him. I'd also ended up with even more questions to answer, and a couple of free bratwursts.

It had definitely been a fruitful ten minutes.

After lunch and a wander round the gardens to work off the sweetcorn and honey ice cream we'd had for dessert, Mark and I went our separate ways. I needed to get on top of my budgets, and while the festival was still on and the cafés were quiet, it was the ideal chance to lock myself away in my office and get them out of the way. If the heat inside my office caused me to sweat off a couple of pounds, then that was an added bonus.

I was pulling up the spreadsheets on my computer when Chelsea stuck her head around the door.

'Sophie, there's a bloke to see you. Bruce someone.'

'Thanks. Er, Chelsea…' I picked up the waste basket from under my desk and held it out to her. 'Chewing gum.'

She rolled her eyes and removed the gum from her mouth. I didn't say anything else; she'd get the idea. I stretched my back out as I stood and took a deep breath; I still wasn't in the right frame of mind to talk to Bruce about ending our business relationship, and anyway, I needed to know exactly what I was going to use instead before I did anything. The last thing I needed was our final few deliveries being late, or being sent the wrong stuff because Bruce was annoyed or just focusing on the customers who were sticking with him. Added to that, I was a coward and was choosing to avoid what was likely to be a difficult conversation.

Bruce Keen from the Northern Bean Company was sitting at the end of a table, tapping his foot madly and picking at a label on the side of the box he had brought with him. He stood up when he saw me coming.

'Sophie, hi, hope I'm not disturbing something.'

'No, it's fine. I'm just surprised to see you, you don't normally make deliveries. Plus it's a Bank Holiday, aren't you meant to be taking the day off?'

He glanced around the room. 'No, no, too much to do, you know how it is. I've brought you the samples I was telling you about.' He patted the box. 'We've added another Ethiopian farm to our list, so I've brought you some of the beans I'm getting from them, both a single and a blend, and then there's a couple of flavoured ones that are kind of fun. A cinnamon and rum one and a toasted coconut.' He pushed the box towards me. 'So how are things here? Are the police still around or have they moved on?'

'A couple of them are still here, but the festival is doing OK.' I wanted to get back to my budgets, so I hoped that short answers would help encourage him out of the door.

'Have the police any idea who did it?'

I shook my head. 'They've not made any arrests as far as I know.'

Bruce nodded. 'Have you heard if they've got any leads? Are they hopeful?'

This was quickly becoming an odd conversation. No chitchat, no talk about the coffee, just straight into the murder. It wasn't like we knew each other well and regularly exchanged gossip.

'I've really no idea, Bruce. I know they've interviewed some of the staff here and a lot of the stallholders, but I'm unlikely to find out what they've discovered, if anything.' That wasn't strictly true. Give him a piece of cake and a coffee, and I could probably wheedle the information out of Joe, but I wasn't planning on telling Bruce that.

'OK, well, I just wondered. I should be going.' He stood and moved the box even closer to me. 'Let me know what you think. We're roasting all this week, so if you like them, I can get a few more boxes out to you by the end of the week.' He paused and I thought for a brief moment that he was going to shake my hand, but instead he turned and walked out. I'd avoided a difficult conversation, but got rather a strange one instead.

'So he was frugal. I'm not sure how that helps us.' Mark was driving me home and I was bringing him up to date on my conversation with Tom. 'Unless this meant he had one enormous debt and he was taking on smaller ones in order to pay off the angriest of his creditors.'

'He could have had a gambling problem, or maybe drugs,' I suggested. I didn't believe either of these ideas; I was just throwing things out there in the hope one of them might stick or trigger an idea.

Mark was clearly thinking along the same lines as me. 'No, nobody has said anything that would indicate that.' He drove slowly through the beautiful Charleton estate, keeping an eye out for any deer coming close to the side of the road. Charleton House was set in 40,000 acres of rolling countryside, the wooded hillsides home to red and fallow deer. There were trout ponds and miles of stunning walks, and in the distance, a church steeple peeped out from between the trees. It was an idyllic English setting that sent the tourists wild, inspired artists and brought a tear to my eye. Moving back here was proving to be the best decision I had ever made.

'Are you looking forward to getting back to normal?'

I looked over at Mark, unsure what he meant. 'Hmm?'

'Now the fair is over, you'll be busy again.'

'Funnily enough, I am. I thought I'd welcome the break, but I enjoy it when we're busy. I have a good team, like a well-oiled machine.'

'So long as you keep greasing the cogs with coffee it will stay that way. Talking of greasing the cogs, do you fancy a drink?' We were pulling into the village and could see the Black Swan up ahead, but I wasn't really in the mood.

'Not tonight, thanks all the same. I think I'm just going to relax, spend a bit of time with Pumpkin, maybe plan some menus.'

'OK, well promise me you'll do it with a gin and tonic in one hand and something unhealthy in the other.'

'A gin and tonic isn't unhealthy?'

'Darling, put a slice of lime in it and it's one of your five a day.'

We were both distracted by the sound of shouting as we neared the pub car park and our heads swivelled in the direction of two men who looked as if they were about to come to blows. Mark slowed down to a crawl, but the men were too focused on trying to hit one another to notice that they had an audience.

As we got nearer, I recognised them. 'That's Guy and Kyle. Can you hear what they're saying?'

Mark wound down his window, but we still couldn't make out what they were shouting at each other over the noise of the engine. Guy was clearly furious; his face was red and he was jumping about as if the tarmac under his feet was red hot. Kyle on the other hand was standing his ground. He looked just as angry, but more in control.

'What was his alibi?' Mark had read my thoughts. Right now, Guy looked angry enough to kill.

'He was with Malcolm, having a breakfast meeting. Although to be fair, they both look angry enough to take a swipe at someone.'

As though he had heard me, Kyle threw his arms up in the air and shook his head. He started to walk towards the rear door of the pub, but Guy grabbed his shoulder and spun him around, his fist raised. I tensed my body, waiting for Guy's fist to make impact, but something stopped him. Guy froze, and Kyle, who had seemed ready to take it, walked calmly inside. Guy stood with his head resting against the stone wall, looking as if he was trying to calm down. After a couple of minutes, he followed Kyle inside.

I'd been so engrossed that I hadn't even noticed that the car had come to a stop. Mark and I looked at each other, wide-eyed.

'Well, that's enough drama for tonight. Are you sure you don't want to go in for a drink, try and find out what was going on?'

I was tempted, but decided against it.

'My guess is they'll go to their rooms and stew for the rest of the night. We're not going to find out anything tonight.' I opened the car door and got out. 'Drive safely, morning coffee in Library?'

'Throw in some chocolate croissants and you have a date.' And with his order placed, Mark drove off. I walked round the corner to my little house and, I was guessing, a grumpy and demanding cat.

Pumpkin was on the mat, waiting for me as I walked in. I was getting home later than she would have liked, or at least that was how I read the expression on her face as I followed her swaying tail into the kitchen and reached for a glass out of the cupboard. This was my first chance to really savour the Twenty Trees Gin that I had bought from the fair, so I was going to take Mark's advice and pour myself a glass of gin and tonic.

Sitting down at the kitchen table, I let Pumpkin jump up onto my lap. I couldn't remember the last time she had been weighed, but I would have sworn she was the same weight as a small child, with the attitude of a haughty teenager under the illusion that the world revolves around them. In Pumpkin's case, it's not an illusion; the world really does revolve around her.

She rubbed her face against my chin, purring, then against the side of my glass. I only narrowly avoided losing its contents. After sticking her claws into my shirt and probably making a number of holes, she considered her duty complete and jumped off my knee to collapse in a heap by my feet. Her large tabby mass spread across the floor until she was the size of the small dog that she seemed to believe she was.

I sat back and put my feet on the chair next to me. Swirling the ice around my glass, I breathed in and liked what I discovered. The drink's grassy notes made me think of fresh country air, hibiscus and lemongrass, maybe a touch of pine. My love of gin wasn't something that I allowed to cross over into work too much; this was for pleasure only, when the working day was over and I could fully relax. Only tonight my mind wouldn't stop whirring. The conversations I'd been having about Ben were buzzing around my brain and showed no signs of quietening down, even under the influence of alcohol.

Taking centre stage right now was the image of Kyle and Guy fighting outside the pub. I couldn't be sure that it was related to Ben's murder; maybe they were under a lot of stress and emotions were simply running high after the death of their colleague. That wasn't hard to imagine. Maybe they had found Ben stealing their profits, killed him in a moment of anger, and then made it look like a robbery to hide their tracks, only now they were worried they were going to get caught and were taking it out on each other. The problem with that idea was that they both had rock-solid alibis. Perhaps the murder *was* the result of a robbery and the guy who had been selling the coffee down the pub was going to find himself serving a life sentence once Joe got hold of him. That I did find hard to believe. You'd have to be pretty stupid to kill someone and then start selling the evidence at a pub under five miles away.

My next thought was of Elliot Forrester, the gardener Mark and I had seen having a go at Ben, having almost barrelled me to the ground. He wasn't afraid of being seen shouting at Ben and had no problem expressing whatever was annoying him, so it didn't seem like there would be unreleased rage simmering inside him, ready to bubble over into violence. At least, not the murderous kind.

But I could look at that another way. A man not afraid of showing his temper in public, not caring what others thought, might just be able to get angry enough to kill someone. After all, he didn't seem to have a self-control button.

Tom Bidwell didn't appear to be carrying any residual anger; instead, he remembered Ben fondly. As far as he was concerned, no one else was baying for Ben's blood over a couple of hundred quid here or there, either. Ben was coming across as an unremarkable man who, with the exception of Elliot, few people felt any ill will towards. None of it seemed to fit easily. It was like a jigsaw puzzle that looked, from a distance, as if all the pieces would slot together, but once you tried to match them, they were misshapen and wouldn't flatten into place.

I looked at my glass. It was empty. That wasn't going to help things. I needed another drink.

With a second drink in my hand, I moved next door to the sitting room and sat on the sofa, opening my laptop on my knee. Pumpkin made a half-hearted attempt to sit on the keypad, but realised for herself it was unworkable before I had to shoo her off. She settled instead for curling up in a ball by my side. Something had been bugging me, and I didn't know if it was connected to anything. It was just there in my mind and I wanted to do something about it.

I'd been wondering about the art theft at Berwick, and then at Charleton House. Joe had said they were very different crimes carried out in different circumstances, but I wanted to check them out anyway. It wasn't because I thought they were connected to Ben, but I felt so bad for the Duke. It was hard to spend any time with him and not realise just how important art was in his life, especially a piece that had meant a lot to his mother. I wondered if I could help, plus my brain would not settle. I was beginning to wish I was into meditation or distracting myself with muscle-aching exercise, but neither of those things were up my alley, so I just had to run with it and see what I could find.

I spent the next hour searching for art thefts from historic houses, focusing on Derbyshire, but taking into account anything in the neighbouring counties. There had been five in Derbyshire over the last six months, and three in neighbouring areas, the bulk of them carried out since April. Then I looked further back in time and found that over the preceding twelve months, there had been eight reported thefts in the area, starting in March and ending in September. That timeline made sense as many historic houses closed over the winter and couldn't be accessed by the public.

I looked at the houses. Some were run by charities, some were privately owned, but all were open to the public at some point during the year. Two of the thefts had been of paintings small enough to be hidden in a bag, the rest were either silverware or ceramics of one kind or another. I couldn't see any pattern of locations or kinds of houses. I even started reading about the history of the houses – maybe there was a connection from centuries ago, but I wasn't finding anything. Adding to this the fact that I was getting my information mainly from press reports, so it could have been that not all the relevant information had been made public, I started to feel like I was wasting my time.

If there were any links, then Joe stood a better chance of finding them than I did. Joe had already given Mark and me far more information than he ever should, and part of me felt guilty that he could get in a lot of trouble if he was found out. Not guilty enough, however, to stop me sending him a text message and promising him fresh chocolate croissants and as much free coffee as he could drink if he came round tomorrow morning before we opened to the public. I was really hoping that under the influence of my baking, he'd forget all pretence of professionalism and bring me up to speed on what he'd found out so far.

CHAPTER 9

'*Y*ou're kidding, right?' Joe looked over at Mark hopefully. 'She is kidding?'

I placed a tray of muffins in front of them, the result of my early arrival at work and a quick baking session before any of my staff arrived. I'd promised Joe and Mark some freshly baked chocolate croissants, which were coming, but first I wanted them to try my latest experiment.

'Chocolate and beetroot muffins?' Mark looked as nonplussed as Joe. 'What would Ruth say? I will tell her.' His threat of revealing my experimentation to our pastry chef wouldn't come to anything. After all, it had been Ruth who'd encouraged me to have fun and try new things when baking.

I decided to ignore Mark's comments. 'The chocolate is produced by a local artisanal chocolatier and the beetroots are from the Duchess's own vegetable garden.' I'd been inspired by the Food Festival and the idea had come to me last night as my online research became a journey down an internet black hole of food ideas. I was pretty impressed with myself; Joe and Mark less so, it seemed, but I put that down to surprise and not having heard of the combination before.

They both reached for a muffin and examined them more closely, then looked at each other like soldiers about to go over the top. I swear they were a heartbeat from a manly pat on the shoulder and a good luck wish. Each took a bite and chewed slowly while looking at me, back at each other, at the muffins, and then back at me again.

Mark swallowed.

'So?' I asked him. I loved the idea of the muffins, and thought that with the backstory of the ingredients, they'd make a great addition to the menus in the Stables and Library Cafés. Mark took a mouthful of coffee, looking as if he was thinking – hard.

'Well, you know how much I love chocolate, and I'm up for trying pretty much anything. The chocolate, yep, great. Those chunks are fabulous, you can tell it's good quality.' He paused and looked over at Joe. 'And I think this is a great example of a project that combines the work of the kitchens and the gardens, largely because it tastes like I've just eaten a mouthful of Charleton's finest artisanal soil.'

Joe sniggered as Mark took another mouthful of coffee and swilled his mouth out with it.

'Sophie, I've become very fond of you, and I love being one of your chief tasters, but please don't pursue this or I might have to resign from my position.'

'They're not that bad, surely?' I reached for a muffin and took an enormous bite. After a couple of chews, I saw his point. I felt like I'd just licked one of the gardeners' spades. 'Oh God, alright, point taken. I can't argue. Can't blame me for trying, though.'

It was Joe's turn to speak up. 'No, you're right, we can't. But we can blame you for trying them out on us. I thought you liked us.'

I laughed at them. 'Oh shut up, the pair of you. I'll go and get the croissants.'

I let them eat a croissant each in silence, the looks on their faces oddly serene.

'Better?' I raised an eyebrow at them, daring them to make a cheeky comeback, but all I got were synchronised 'mmmms' and a 'God, yes' from Mark. Deciding that I had Joe in a moment of chocolate-induced weakness, I enquired after the murder investigation and how it was going.

'Slowly,' he answered. 'We just can't get hold of anything concrete. Friends, family, they all say the same thing about him: a nice guy who couldn't get any real purchase on life. I've spoken to a bunch of people he owed money to, but none of them seem particularly angry. They're just really sorry he's been killed. I guess that's the thing about small town life: he's one of theirs and they care about that more than a couple of hundred quid. It's a reminder of why I like it round here. There's so much awful stuff going on in the world, but they seem to have their priorities straight.'

His comment about money reminded me of my conversation with Tom. 'From what I've heard, there wasn't much evidence of him spending the money he borrowed, or earned for that matter. Any idea what was going on? Was he gambling?'

'Who have you been talking to?' Joe looked both curious and slightly annoyed. As he'd finished his croissant, it seemed the window on his moment of weakness had closed. 'You shouldn't be getting involved, Sophie. I've already told you far too much. You need to leave this to the police.'

'It was just a couple of locals who were working at the festival. We got chatting about Ben. It's a hard subject to avoid when he was killed right here and many of them knew him.'

That seemed to placate him, but he did pause for a moment before replying.

'We haven't found evidence of gambling. He seemed to travel quite a bit with the job, but mainly around Derbyshire. Sometimes further north in England – presumably the company covered his expenses for that.'

'What about the lad Tina saw selling coffee in The Old Oak?'

Mark asked. I hadn't realised that he'd been paying attention; I'd assumed he was still in a croissant-shaped world of his own.

Joe smiled, his lecture forgotten. 'Local lad was romancing his girlfriend in the back of his car in a layby north of here. They got out to have a smoke and he found the coffee abandoned in the grass.'

Mark snorted. 'And they say romance is dead. Presumably the sweet Juliet can confirm her Romeo's story?'

'She certainly can. We also found a couple of bags they'd missed when we visited the site. Problem is, we can't know if the lad selling them knew they were stolen goods, so it will be difficult to prove any kind of offence. Either way, it doesn't help our investigation at all.'

Talk of Romeo and Juliet got me thinking. 'Did Ben have a girlfriend, or boyfriend? Maybe this is the work of an aggrieved partner.'

'You still fancy the crime of passion route? No, not that we can find. He lived a pretty quiet life with his mum when he wasn't on the road. He has a brother down in London he phoned occasionally, a few friends he'd go to the pub with. We did find a picture of a kid in his wallet, but his mum didn't recognise her and thinks she might belong to a friend of his. She said he was always good with youngsters and got quite attached to his friends' children – a sort of honorary uncle.'

'He sounds a bit too good to be true,' Mark commented. 'He has to have had a murky side hidden away for someone to have killed him.'

I wasn't sure I agreed. I'd heard enough stories from Mark over the last year to know that history was littered with innocent victims.

'Think about all the research you've done. There must be countless people who have been wrongly accused of things, or became the target of treacherous kings and noblemen just because they were in the way of their dastardly ambitions.'

'Fair enough.' In the silence that followed, Mark stared into his mug, and then looked up, his puppy dog eyes sending a clear message. I reached out for his mug.

'You really need to work on your subtlety. Joe, more coffee?'

'No thanks, I should be going. I need to head back to Berwick Hall – a member of staff I need to interview about the theft has just returned from holiday. I'm hoping I can get something from him that is tantamount to a lead; that's another case that's grinding along far too slowly.'

I held the plate of muffins out towards him. 'One for the road?' A look of mock horror appeared on his face and, with wide eyes, he pretended to sprint for the door, stopping briefly to wave before he disappeared.

'You'll never see him again,' was Mark's response. 'Wave those things at me and I'll run for the hills too.'

I couldn't resist.

After sending Mark on his way, clearing up our coffee mugs and finding precisely no one who wanted me to add chocolate and beetroot muffins to the menu, I wandered off to the events team office so Yeshim could give me the run down on a corporate booking. Nothing hugely exciting: the board members of a local art gallery were holding their annual away day here at Charleton House. It was their chance to discuss profit and loss and future exhibition sponsorship underneath a chandelier that would kill if it fell on them, in a room with a view that would take their breath away. I was providing the refreshments, among them a buffet lunch that included a beetroot salad – I was determined to get beetroot in somewhere.

After a brief conversation, I left Yeshim to it when she got a phone call from a bridezilla from hell who was holding her wedding here in the autumn. As I left the office, I made a mental note to return with cake for the worn-down looking events manager. I sensed that she was going to need it.

Ambling down the private lane, enjoying the warmth of the

sunshine and exchanging pleasantries with staff I passed on my way, I spotted a familiar figure walking towards me: Guy Glover. He had the swagger of a man with a lot of confidence who always liked what he saw in the mirror.

'Morning, Sophie,' he called out once he'd spotted me. 'Getting some fresh air?' He clearly had no idea that I'd witnessed his fight with Kyle. Either that, or he didn't care.

'Something like that. What about you? The festival is over, so why are you still here?'

'I have some paperwork to drop off with Yeshim. I wanted to get everything squared off before we move on to the next event.'

'Does that mean the police have given you the van back?'

'No, not yet, and to be honest, I don't think we'll use it again. We'll sell it and invest in a new one. I'll admit to not being overly sentimental, but I have my limits. I don't think anyone wants to stand serving coffee where... well, you know what I mean. I'm sure I can find someone who will take it off my hands for a reasonable price. They're worth a lot of money, and if a buyer isn't aware of its more recent history, then I'm sure I can get a decent amount for it.'

I'd gone from impressed by an apparent display of feelings to appalled by how quickly he'd turned the conversation to making money out of someone's ignorance about Ben's murder. I hadn't been sure before, but now I knew I didn't like him, and I decided I wasn't going to be shy about last night.

'I saw you at the pub yesterday. You and Kyle didn't seem to be getting on very well.'

He looked momentarily confused, then realised what I was referring to.

'You saw that? I didn't spot you.'

'You wouldn't have done. We were driving past and you were a bit preoccupied.' He wedged his hands firmly in his pockets and looked uncomfortable. 'Do you and Kyle often argue like that?'

He gave an awkward laugh. 'It was nothing. We argue all the

time. I've known Kyle since he was sixteen, so I guess he's like a brother to me. We have a bit of rough and tumble every now and then; next thing we're happily having a pint together.' He was clearly growing in confidence, and when he laughed again, it sounded a lot less awkward. 'We'll probably have another argument in a week or two. Hopefully you won't have to witness it next time, though.'

He smiled as though we were in on a great joke together. I wasn't falling for it.

'It must have been pretty serious to cause an actual fight, though. You seemed really mad at him.'

He looked away briefly, and then turned back to face me.

'It really was nothing, Sophie. You don't need to give it another moment's thought. Now, I need to make sure I catch Yeshim, then I have a diary full of appointments.'

Before I had a chance to say anything else, he walked off. 'Take care, Sophie, see you next year,' he shouted over his shoulder as he strode away at great speed, making sure our conversation couldn't continue. While it might be over for him, I knew he was lying, so as far as I was concerned, this was far from over for me.

CHAPTER 10

You might think that a dark room with walls covered in shelves groaning under the weight of thousands of books, dark leather armchairs and dark wood tables all around would be the last place you'd want to spend time on a warm summer's day, but no matter what was going on outside, I always found the Library Café comfortable and welcoming. In the winter, it was a cosy escape from the worst of the weather; in the summer, it transformed into a cool respite from the sun's rays. I had yet to find a season in which this wasn't my favourite of the three cafés.

Today it seemed like the visitors agreed. With the Food Festival packing up and the stallholders moving on, the visitors had returned to the cafés for lunch and their restorative coffee and cake. Staff members also reappeared in their droves for a caffeine-fuelled pick-me-up before meetings; others held their meetings in here with coffee and cake to make it all the more bearable. Visitors would browse the shelves, taking in the selection of books that the Duke had demanded would not merely be decoration, but would reflect the interests and history of the house and generations of the family that had lived here. Art, architecture, gardening, social history, Shakespeare – books of all kinds were there on the walls of the café, sourced from second-hand bookshops throughout Derbyshire, giving visitors a glimpse into the minds of the Fitzwilliam-Scotts. It amazed me that so few books were stolen, but the first time I'd mentioned to the Duke that there *were* some gaps on the shelves, he'd simply smiled and said he hoped that the books gave their new owners great pleasure.

I had spent the morning helping to keep the shelves of sandwiches stocked, serving iced coffee and clearing tables. It was a day for mucking in and I didn't mind; it was a nice change from spreadsheets and emails, and anyway, my office was unbearably hot and I'd grab any excuse to stay out of there. I'd just finished advising a couple of American visitors on what I felt were the 'must see' parts of the house and was wiping down tables when Kathy Wright came in. She looked tired and distracted, but smiled when she spotted me.

'Hi, Kathy, lovely to see you. Can I get you a coffee, or is that not the generous offer it sounds?'

She laughed. 'I wouldn't say no. My morning cup just doesn't seem to be enough today.' Despite the smile that had crossed her face, she still looked tired. Her eyes flitted around the café, unable to settle on me, or anything else for that matter. 'I'm actually here to drop this off for you while Lucy is up at the events office with Yeshim. We thought you might like some more samples, have a chance to try some of the coffee that we didn't have on sale at the festival.'

Kathy handed me a cardboard box. I opened it to find six beautifully packaged sample bags with the adorable Signal Box logo printed on every one.

'What a wonderful surprise, you've made my day. Grab a seat and I'll be back with the coffee.'

After stashing the box of coffee in my office – there was no way I wanted anyone accidentally serving the samples along with our usual stuff – I made two cups of coffee using some of the sample Kathy and Lucy had given me over the weekend and went to sit down with her.

'Are you all packed up now?'

'We are. We drove the van straight off last night. It's so easy to pack up and go; it's one of the things we love about it.'

We sat in uncomfortable silence for a moment or two while Kathy played with sachets of sugar. I was struggling to find anything to say that wasn't pure business and this didn't seem like the time. Kathy must have had enough of that over the weekend.

'Was it a success for you?'

'Hmm, sorry?' She looked at me blankly

'The festival, was it a success for you?'

'Yes. It was the first one at Charleton House we'd been part of and we'll definitely come again.'

'Well, I'm glad to hear that Ben's murder hasn't put you off.'

She picked up another packet of sugar and started folding it in her fingers. I couldn't stand it anymore and didn't care that I hardly knew the woman.

'Look, Kathy, I don't mean to intrude, but is everything alright? When I first met you on Friday, you seemed really happy to be here, but I haven't seen you smile once over the weekend. Well, not while I've been around, and I'm wondering if I should take it personally or if there's something wrong I can help with. I hardly know you, but I like you and your sister, and I'd like to do some business with you, so it would be good for us to get off on the right foot and have clear air between us.'

Kathy looked up, surprised. 'Oh God, no, it's not you, or the fair, or the house. This whole weekend has been great. I just, well…' – she glanced around the room – 'I did something really stupid, and if my sister finds out, I don't think she'll react well. We've put our hearts and souls into this business, and I don't want to screw it up, but I think I might have done.'

She looked genuinely worried as, for the first time, she looked directly at me.

'I have no idea why I'm telling you this; I hardly know you.' She stopped and took a deep breath. 'Friday night, a few of us had gone to the pub after we'd finished setting up. The Black Swan, just down the road. Well, Lucy went home early. She wanted to get a good night's sleep, but I stayed for another drink. I ended up sat with Guy from Silver Bullet. One thing led to another and, well, I spent the night with him. That wouldn't be a big deal, but he's the competition and someone that neither Lucy nor I have a lot of respect for professionally. I was an idiot after a couple of drinks too many and Lucy is going to kill me.

'Of course, it also made it awkward for the rest of the weekend. He attempted to get me alone a couple of times. He seemed to give up fairly quickly and didn't try anything on, or really say anything, but he had a knowing look in his eye, like he had something he could use against me. He's a bit of a sleaze.'

She sat back in her chair. I didn't know why she'd just told me all that, either, but if it helped her, then I was OK with it. I remembered the live interpretation with Samuel Pepys on Sunday morning when Guy had followed Kathy into the room. She'd been trying to avoid him. He, on the other hand, had looked rather amused by it all.

'You need to talk to your sister. There's no way she doesn't know something is bothering you. If I could tell, then she will. You're never going to be able to move on from this if you don't talk to her. You're bound to end up at the same events as Guy for years to come.'

She nodded. 'I know, I'm being ridiculous. I was just so mad at myself; I'm not a one-night stand kind of girl, and the one time I actually do it, it's with him. It creeps me out just thinking about it.' The more she talked, the more emboldened she became. Her voice had stopped sounding so weary and downtrodden, and she was looking me in the eyes again. It seemed that unburdening herself had made a difference.

I decided to dig a bit deeper. 'Did you see Ben before you went up to Guy's room?'

She thought about it for a moment. 'No, he wasn't at the pub. He said he was going to join us, but I didn't see him. Guy went up first and I followed a couple of minutes later, we didn't want to make it obvious. He might have arrived after that and spent time with Kyle or the others.'

My gut told me she was telling the truth. 'What time did you leave in the morning?'

'About five. I wanted to get home and make it look like I'd just gone to bed late, be there when Lucy got up, so I crept out like a guilty teenager.' She shook her head at her own behaviour, then looked directly at me. 'Why the questions? My messed up love life can't be of that much interest to you.'

I was about to answer with some vague version of the truth when I saw Lucy walk into the café and scan the room. She smiled and waved as she walked over.

I looked back at Kathy. 'This is your chance to come clean. I'll get you both a drink.'

I stood up and said hello to Lucy as she joined us, then made two cups of coffee and plated up a couple of chocolate brownies and took them over to the table.

'Are you not joining us?' Lucy enquired as she reached for a brownie.

'I've got a couple of things I need to do, I'll be back in a bit.'

With that, I left them to their heart to heart and kept myself busy. The visitors were still arriving in a steady flow, and the café hummed to the sound of their chatter as I fetched more cakes to put on display. A small child was running between the tables, so I scanned the room, trying to identify his parents, and noticed two women in the far corner. One had a child on her lap, the other an empty pushchair next to her. They were engrossed in something on a phone, scrolling through photos and laughing, taking no interest at all in where the young boy was.

As I asked the boy what his teddy bear was called, one of the women looked over. I pointed at her and with a big smile encouraged the lad to go back to her, but once he reached her, my smile disappeared and I made sure his mother realised I wasn't overly pleased. I love kids; I'd just rather not go flying over one when I'm carrying a pile of dishes or a bowl of hot soup.

After telling a couple of old ladies from Yorkshire which part of the gardens were my favourite as they didn't have much time and wanted to know where they should head first, I helped a father attempt to convince his teenage daughter that this was one of the coolest buildings in the country and she'd get some amazing photos for social media. (I'm not sure we succeeded.) Next I had to ask a grumpy looking bloke to stop manhandling the sandwiches if he wasn't going to buy them. When he reluctantly apologised, I accepted his apology with mildly sarcastic grace.

'It's OK, I'm used to telling children to stop doing it all the time.'

After a while, I was able to slow down and look over to where Kathy and Lucy were sitting. Lucy had hold of her sister's hands and was smiling; Kathy looked incredibly relieved. Suddenly they both laughed. It looked as if all had been forgiven, not that I was sure there had been much to forgive. I was relieved that Kathy seemed genuinely not to have seen Ben on Friday night, so if he had seen her going into Guy's room, she wasn't aware. For a moment, I wondered if Ben had caught up with Kathy later and threatened to blackmail her. It seemed he was always in need of money, but I couldn't think when she would have seen him if she had left the pub at 5am, and by 8am he was dead. No, she could be ruled out, I was sure of that.

Once it became clear that Kathy and Lucy's discussion had become more light-hearted, I made my way over.

'Mind if I join you?' A daft question as I'd just turned up with three coffees.

'Of course not.' Lucy pulled out a chair for me. I looked across at Kathy, who smiled at me in a way I hadn't seen since Friday. She looked so much more relaxed.

'We were just trying to predict what you might want to talk to us about,' Kathy said with a glint in her eye. I imagined that they already had a pretty good idea.

'Probably not hard to guess, but why don't we go back a bit and you tell me more about the company.'

Kathy indicated towards her sister, allowing Lucy to start talking.

'Well, like we said, our grandfather had a replica signal box at the bottom of his garden. He'd worked on the railways all his life and he loved it. He built the signal box when we were only small, so I don't remember a time when it wasn't there. It had two floors. The ground floor was used as a garden shed, but above that was where we loved to go as kids. He had a model railway set up there – it was incredible. He'd made all the little buildings and landscaped it to look like part of Derbyshire. He'd recreated the Edale Valley and some of its stations. It was beautiful. He used to make up stories about the people on the trains and the little figures at the stations.'

Lucy looked across the table at her sister and I noticed that they had exactly the same smiles. As they looked at each other, I guessed they were picturing the same scene and recalling the same memories.

Kathy continued. 'Our grandmother had died when we were tiny and he was devastated. They were so in love. The model railway was his distraction; he spent most of his time down there. I don't think he was trying to forget; the opposite, in fact. He was always telling us stories about her. There were pictures of them together on the walls. I'm sure he talked to her when we weren't there.'

She paused for a moment, then took a deep breath.

'When he died and left the house to us, Lucy and I decided to move in together. We were both renting small flats in Sheffield and couldn't afford to buy property. This way we had our own place, could save money and eventually do something we'd always talked about doing.'

Lucy raised her coffee mug to me. 'It was our dad who got us into coffee. He isn't hugely knowledgeable about it, but he always started his day with a big mug of coffee. As soon as we were old enough, he taught us how to make it just the way he liked it: a large pot in a French press and a jug of cream. We thought it was a huge honour to be shown how to make it, like we were finally adults.' She laughed. 'Of course, it actually meant we could make him coffee whenever he wanted it.'

'Even take it to him and mum in bed on a weekend.' Kathy rolled her eyes. 'Only instead of resenting it, we started to try and make the perfect coffee. After a while, we would take them new things. We bought different kinds of coffee, made it using different methods, and before long we were obsessed.

'Fast forward fifteen years and we'd moved into our grandfather's house and saved to buy a coffee roaster of our own. We knew exactly where it would go and what we'd call our company. Lucy kept working for a few months and then went part time, but I quit my job and read everything I could get my hands on. I did a few courses and travelled to Ethiopia, Kenya, India. We don't make much money at the moment, but Lucy has been able to join me full time now and we're getting a lot of attention with the van at festivals, so business is picking up.'

Kathy spoke with such passion. Once she had finished talking, I knew I wanted to work with her and her sister.

'So, how would you like to gain another customer and supply the coffee to one of the country's finest historic houses?'

The two sisters looked at each other, their eyes wide. Lucy was the first to speak.

'We thought this might be what you were going to say, but… well, now you've said it out loud, wow! Yeah, of course. That's amazing.'

Kathy threw her head back and laughed. 'Oh my God, suppliers to Charleton House. It's incredible.' She leaned over and flung her arms around me. I wasn't expecting it and nearly fell off my chair, but I hugged her back. She was a different woman to the one I'd seen over the weekend.

'But don't you need to check with the Duke and Duchess?' Lucy asked, looking concerned.

'No, the Duchess never drinks coffee so wouldn't be able to offer an opinion, and the Duke would never get involved with this level of detail. I sometimes run menus past them for their own events, but in the main they leave food- and drink-related decisions up to me.'

'I feel like we should be drinking something other than coffee.' Lucy stared into her empty mug.

'Don't worry, we will,' I replied. 'We'll get the details sorted, then we'll crack open the champagne. But for now, cheers.'

I offered them my mug, they raised theirs, and in a chorus of 'cheers' we saluted our new venture.

After I'd said goodbye to Lucy and Kathy, I made my way through to the kitchen. The café had quietened down and I felt I could leave my extremely competent team to it, so I tidied up the kitchen to look less like a bombsite and started to lay out some ingredients. Following the magnificent fail of the chocolate and beetroot muffins, I wanted another go at experimenting, only this time with a much safer recipe.

After coffee, my favourite liquid to drink is gin – only much less liberally, of course – and I'd had an idea. I was about to get started when there was a loud rapping at the window, so I looked up and found myself face to face with Malcolm. I'd forgotten all about him and it was quite nice to see him. He wasn't someone

I'd choose to socialise with, but he was always friendly and upbeat.

I opened the window.

'Hello, Sophie, hope I'm not disturbing you?'

'Not at all, I was just about to experiment. What are you up to?'

'Not much, stretching my legs. I'm on my way to say goodbye to the Duke and Duchess; I'm heading off shortly.'

'I thought you were staying all week.'

'I was, but something came up in Paris. I'm getting the Eurostar later today, so sadly my little break has been curtailed. It was lovely while it lasted, if a little lively. Is murder a common event around here?'

He laughed, a deep throaty laugh that I imagined being formed by long nights with whisky and cigars.

'Fortunately not.' I decided not to tell him about a murder that had taken place a couple of months earlier. 'It certainly livens things up a bit, though.'

He leaned through the window. 'What delights are you whipping up, or is it top secret?'

'Not at all: gin and tonic cupcakes. I thought they'd be rather nice for some of the events we hold. The Duchess has a few coming up with "ladies who lunch" types, and with it being summer...'

'Sounds delicious. Shame I won't be here long enough to try them, although I'm more of a whisky man myself. Mind you, cake of any kind hits the spot.' He had stepped back from the window and patted his stomach. 'As you can see.'

As he gave another of his throaty laughs, I remembered his meeting with Guy and his interest in restaurants.

'I believe food is a professional interest as well?'

'In what way?'

'I might have got it wrong, but I thought I heard someone say you were interested in opening up a restaurant. Guy is advising you?'

'A restaurant?' He thought briefly. 'Oh yes, of course. Well, not so much opening one myself, but investing in one back in Paris. I don't know much about it so I do a bit of research whenever I can. Guy's done this kind of thing in the past.'

A restaurant in Paris. It all sounded rather romantic, but then anything associated with Paris ended up sounding romantic.

'What sort of food? I ran a couple of restaurants in London over the years, I might be able to help. I'm happy to give you my email address.'

He looked a little flustered; embarrassed, perhaps. Maybe it was a project he was trying to keep secret until more had been confirmed. I was exactly the same way; I hadn't told any of my friends or family about the job at Charleton House until I'd been offered it and accepted.

'Well, it's sort of a mix. Fusion, I guess you'd call it. We're still playing with ideas. Well, the chef is. As the owner, I'd just be the backing.'

He didn't seem very sure. I was used to working with chefs who had a very distinctive style, but I knew that wasn't always the way.

'Whereabouts in Paris will be it? It must have been hard to decide, there are so many beautiful neighbourhoods.'

'Absolutely.' It was as though he hadn't heard my question. 'Well, sorry to say I ought to be getting off. I want to say goodbye to the Duke and Duchess.' He was stepping back from the window as he spoke. 'It's been an absolute delight, Sophie, hope to see you when I next stop by.'

With that, he was off up the lane and out of sight.

I made a start on measuring out the ingredients for the cupcakes, pouring in the two tablespoons of gin the recipe called for, then I reconsidered. I was much more comfortable with the sound of four tablespoons. When it came to boozy cakes, too much was a risk I was always prepared to take. As I worked, I pondered over Malcolm's obvious anxiety to get away from me. What was it with men avoiding conversations? Both Malcolm and Guy had been keen to escape my company as quickly as possible. Maybe I'd made them uncomfortable. Maybe my questions were just a little too close to the bone.

CHAPTER 11

Unusually for England, the hot weather wasn't showing any signs of letting up, so the next morning I welcomed the opportunity to escape my kitchens and head off into the Derbyshire countryside. My car windows were wound down and fresh air buffeted me as I blasted my way round the country lanes. I had spent the morning visiting one of my suppliers, a farm about twenty miles away that supplied all the bacon and sausages I used at Charleton House. It had turned out that the farmer was a bit of a history buff and enjoyed playing with interesting sausage recipes, and I'd been selling one that combined pork, beef, sage and nutmeg. Simple, but delicious and authentic, it had ensured I'd sold record numbers of sausage barms – or sandwiches – to staff in particular. Once I'd arrived, it had been fun to put on my wellies and get a short tour of his farm. The packet of sausages that were now sitting in a cooler in the boot of my car, destined for my own fridge, were a nice bonus.

I swung the car round the tight bends, past farms and cottages selling honey and jams at their gate with an honesty box for money. The cottage gardens held wonderful displays of foxgloves, sweet peas and delphiniums that sang 'English country garden'. Their scents wafted in through my window and I slowed down to admire them, their delicate pinks and cream colours easy on the eye.

I crossed over some train tracks, drove down a steep hill and passed the sign for an industrial estate that was hidden in some trees down a lane. One of the company names on the notice board caught my eye: 'Silver Bullet Coffee Roasters'. Of course, this was where Guy and Kyle had based their company and roasting operation. I wondered idly if they would all be at work, roasting more beans for their next event. In a split second I decided to turn the car round and drop in unannounced. It would be easy for me to claim I was interested in their operation. It wasn't too far away from the truth, and maybe I would find out something more about Ben.

I drove slowly down the pot-holed lane and eventually came to a large clearing. There were five industrial buildings and a number of cars, vans and trucks scattered about, the red-brick walls and metal roofs of the buildings a million miles away from the artistic splendour and show of wealth that the architects of Charleton House had created. I drove slowly past them, looking for one that had a sign referencing coffee.

There it was, on the third building along, next to some external stairs. I parked up the car and got out just as a man appeared from a large open door a few feet away.

'Can I help you, love?'

'I'm looking for Silver Bullet Coffee, I'm guessing they're up there?' I pointed up the metal staircase.

'Sure are. I saw one of them around earlier, but he left about half an hour ago. Why don't you wait upstairs? If he's coming back, it'll be open. I'm guessing you'll be able to make yourself a coffee.'

He laughed at his own joke as I climbed up the metal staircase to the door at the top. The man had been right: the door was unlocked and I let myself in, calling out as I entered, not wanting to take anyone by surprise if it turned out someone was still in there.

No response.

The Silver Bullet offices consisted of two large rooms, connected by a single door. The white walls shone as the sunlight bounced around the room. A couple of desks along one wall held a few untidy piles of paperwork and cables where laptops would be plugged in when someone was working there. On the opposite side of the room was a long, tall shelving unit, filled with cardboard boxes. A couple of the boxes were open and I could see they contained the bags that would go on to hold the Silver Bullet Coffee beans. A few of the empty coffee bags had fallen on the floor; a couple littered one of the desks. There were brown flecks here and there on the pale grey carpet, and the occasional pile of brown powder. I bent down to investigate more closely and realised it was coffee granules.

It made sense. Some customers wanted beans they could grind at home, others wanted them ready ground, avoiding the fuss of that extra step. I for one always ground the coffee myself; I enjoyed playing an additional part in the process of getting the coffee into my cup, and it meant the room filled with the wonderful aroma of fresh beans.

It looked as if the Silver Bullet guys packaged the coffee in here. I stepped through the door, expecting to see the roasting machine in pride of place and waiting to get to work on another batch, but there was nothing. No roaster; no sacks of coffee beans waiting to go in; no sign of a coffee operation at all. But I could tell from indentations on the carpet that large boxes had recently been stored in here, and there were some coffee beans scattered about.

It didn't make any sense. I knew that this was Silver Bullet's registered office and warehouse; I'd looked the company up online as I often did with independent coffee roasters I came across. A small company like this wouldn't be able to afford multiple locations, and if Guy and Kyle had a backer who did enable them to expand, they would have also had the money to make these rooms look a lot more welcoming. There wasn't even a cheap inspirational poster on the wall, let alone empty coffee sacks with interesting designs framed and turned into art. I'd have expected maps of the world that showed where the beans had come from, perhaps a large version of their logo proudly displayed on the front door, but there wasn't any of that here. Yes, there were all the bags that would later be filled with the coffee, but that was it.

The offices were beginning to look like somewhere that had been abandoned in a hurry, like the company had collapsed, the bailiffs had been in, and Guy and Kyle could no longer pay the rent on the space and had just walked out. But I knew that wasn't the case. They had a beautiful Airstream that they took around the country, an employee in the form of Ben – well, an ex-employee – and they were selling their reasonable if uninspired coffee very successfully. I was sure these rooms had not been abandoned. Besides which, the man I had spoken to outside had said that one of them had been here this morning. None of it made any sense.

Returning to the first room, I started to flick through the paperwork on the desk. I was a bit unnerved by how little guilt I felt about that; I wasn't sure if that made me a great snoop or a great detective! There were the usual letters from events companies about upcoming festivals, late payment letters for the rental of this industrial unit, and delivery notes for the boxes on the shelves. There was the receipt for the Airstream, which had been paid off in one lump sum twelve months ago. There was also paperwork relating to the Sheffield Roasting Hub. I'd heard of it before, but I quickly pulled the information up on my phone to refresh my memory.

The Sheffield Roasting Hub was a coffee roasting facility

where people could rent the space by the half day and roast their own coffee using the equipment provided. It was a great solution for small companies that couldn't afford the huge financial investment of buying their own roasting equipment. I pulled some of the paperwork together – it looked as if Silver Bullet had stopped using the Roasting Hub roughly twelve months ago. That would usually mean that a company had finally been able to afford its own equipment, but not Silver Bullet. Or at least, there was no sign of it here.

What were Guy and Kyle playing at? They weren't using the Roasting Hub, they hadn't bought their own equipment, and yet they had the money to buy an enormous, gleaming Airstream. The more unusual it seemed, the more uncomfortable I started to feel, and I decided it was time to leave.

As I turned towards the door, I spotted a small piece of card on the floor. It was a business card for Bruce Keen from the Northern Bean Company. I was now doubly confused as I couldn't imagine what Bruce had been doing here, unless he was planning on going into business with Guy and Kyle, which I found unlikely. One of the attractions for customers to companies like Silver Bullet was their independence and small-scale operation. Mind you, without any equipment, Silver Bullet's operation was so small it was virtually non-existent.

I stepped back out into the summer heat and down the stairs, my footsteps making the metal steps clang as I went. Next to the stairs was a large metal skip and I glanced inside as I went down, using my temporary bird's-eye view. There were dozens of empty folded cardboard boxes inside. I was hoping that the Silver Bullet lads were planning on recycling them when I spotted something familiar on the side of one of the boxes. It was an image of a pile of coffee beans with three letters underneath: 'NBC' – the logo for The Northern Bean Company.

I stopped a couple of steps from the bottom of the stairs and stared at the boxes. Silver Bullet's coffee had tasted exactly like that of NBC – I'd used the same words to describe them both. That was because they *were* the same.

Silver Bullet Coffee and NBC coffee were one and the same.

As I stood there, staring into the skip, it all became clear. Guy and Kyle were decanting NBC coffee into Silver Bullet branded bags and selling it as their own, with a healthy mark up on the price because people were happy to pay more when they thought they were supporting a small local company. I was horrified by what they were doing, and I couldn't help but wonder if this had some bearing on Ben's murder. Was Ben in on it to the same extent as Guy and Kyle, assuming, of course, that as the owners of the company, Guy and Kyle were both happily behind this idea? Had Ben been supportive of the scheme, or was he a reluctant participant, in it solely to keep his job? Had he developed a conscience about what they were doing and been threatening to blow the whistle on the whole operation? That of course would put Guy and Kyle directly in the spotlight as having motives.

On the other hand, Bruce must have been furious when he realised what was happening. I was sure he would have put it together in the same way I had. When had he visited and dropped the business card? I knew he'd been in the area on Friday and Saturday – surely this now gave him a motive.

I started to feel distinctly vulnerable. The last thing I needed were any potential killers turning up and discovering that I was in on their secret, so I went back to my car. I was about forty minutes' drive from Charleton House and that would give me some thinking time; I'd call Joe when I was back at the office.

The route from the industrial estate to Charleton House took me past my home and the Black Swan Pub. I'd already decided on my next plan of action and I pulled into the car park.

There were a few customers sitting in the beer garden, enjoying the sunshine and an early afternoon pint as I went in. It was nice to get inside, my eyes welcoming the rest after the glare of the sunshine, especially as I'd left my sunglasses in my office. I looked about for the landlord and found him wiping down a table in the far corner.

'Steve, do you have a minute?'

'Of course, can I get you a drink?'

'No thanks, I can't stop. This is going to be a bit of an odd question, but you know the two guys from the coffee company that have been staying here? Well, one of them was here for breakfast the day of the murder up at the house. Do you remember him?'

'Of course, Kyle. The police were asking about him.'

'Do you remember what time he left?'

'Sure. Like I told the police, I saw him leave at about nine. I remember because I had a delivery arrive as he was leaving and the brewery is always dead on time. Sorry, that's not a good way of putting it under the circumstances.'

I smiled so he knew he hadn't offended me.

'That was quite late for breakfast.'

'He wasn't eating breakfast that late; he had it delivered to his room at seven. We started doing room service about six months ago. Just for breakfast, mind, and it's been really popular. He did that each morning he was here. I took the tray up to his room at seven, then collected the dirty dishes after I saw him leave at nine.'

We'd moved over to the bar and Steve started emptying a dishwasher as we spoke. The hot steam from the machine hit me in the face and I stepped back.

'Sorry, luv, I should have warned you.'

I removed my glasses and wiped the steam from them. 'Did you tell the police that?'

'What, that he ate in his room?' He thought for a moment, and then shook his head. 'No, they wanted to know if he'd had breakfast here and what time he'd left, so that's what I told them. Is everything OK?'

I didn't want to give too much away; I had no idea if Steve was one of those gossipy landlords who enjoy knowing everyone's business and coming across as the fount of all knowledge, so I kept my feelings to myself.

'Everything's fine, thanks, I just wanted to check. See you soon.' After promising to return for a drink as soon as possible, I jumped back in the car, noting exactly what time I set off. I wanted to be 100% sure how long it took me to get back up to the house.

'So you think he might have snuck out after he'd had his breakfast delivered, killed Ben, and then returned so he could be seen leaving the pub later on?'

I was sitting in my stuffy office with the door closed, beads of sweat running down my forehead. I felt sticky and disgusting, but I had to make sure no one could overhear my phone conversation with Joe. To be extra sure, I'd turned the dishwasher on in the kitchen. The noise drowned out any conversation that escaped under the door, but it just added to the heat. At this rate I was going to sweat off a few pounds – no bad thing.

'It's possible. It took me nine minutes to drive from the pub to the car park. Kyle had two hours from the point of breakfast being delivered to being seen leaving the pub. You said that Ben had been murdered around about 8am. That gives Kyle loads of time to get here, argue with Ben, kill him and get back.'

'True.' Joe didn't sound entirely convinced. 'But how did he manage it without appearing on camera? The car park is almost fully covered, and if he took the route stallholders take to get to their stalls, he'd definitely have been seen. And the security staff would have had to sign him in anyway. Nobody said anything about seeing him.'

He had a point, but I wasn't giving up that easily. 'Kyle grew up around here, which means he probably knew the estate reasonably well and knew how to get in and out unseen. Most locals have walked the estate countless times over the years, and they drive through here regularly. It's not uncommon for the security team to find some drunken teenagers daring each other to climb over walls and go for a dip in the Great Pond.'

'And his motive?' Joe didn't sound like he was completely dismissing my theory. If anything, I imagined he was annoyed with the police officers who had interviewed Steve and not got the details about Kyle having breakfast in his room, out of sight of anyone else: a distinctly less watertight alibi than they had previously believed.

'Kyle and Guy are passing off someone else's coffee as their own. It means they have considerably less overheads as they haven't had to buy a roaster. They're not paying the costs associated with running it and they're not dealing with the hassle of importing beans. They're repackaging someone else's coffee, marking up the price and selling it for a decent profit. Buying expensive locally produced products is all the rage now. You should have seen the prices at some of the stalls over the weekend, and yet people were still happily handing over their cash. It wouldn't take much to run, and Kyle and Guy could have been leaving Ben to do all the work, while they're off making more money through other business ventures.'

There was silence on the other end as Joe took in what I was saying.

'None of this is without logic, Sophie, but I just don't know how Kyle could have got in and out of the gardens without being spotted by someone. The gardens team, for example – there were about half a dozen of them preparing for the start of the festival, and many of them had been onsite since 6am and were working within the vicinity of the festival stalls. But none of them saw anything out of the ordinary. It would have made more sense for

Elliot to have done it. He was actually meant to be in the gardens at that time, but he has an alibi too.

'I'll talk to DS Harnby and we'll get someone over to the industrial estate. At the very least, Kyle and Guy are going to have to answer some awkward questions from the Trading Standards Office about how they run their business, and they're bound to wind up in court over that. And you're right, if Ben got tired of how they were doing business, then both Kyle and Guy have suddenly got a substantial motive for wanting him out of the way. But alibis and access to the gardens are problematic. Leave it with me.'

'There's something else you ought to be aware of as well.' As I told Joe about Bruce's business card and that he probably knew about the scam, I heard him breathe out, hard. I could imagine him leaning back in his chair and messing with his hair as he thought about what I'd told him; I'd seen him do it before when he was taken by surprise. He didn't seem to realise doing it would leave his hair in a straggly mess, but it was rather endearing nonetheless.

'Well that's a new one. I'll add it to my list of things for DS Harnby... Thanks, I owe you.' I'd yet to meet her, but I knew that Detective Sergeant Harnby was proving to be a tough, though fair, boss, so I was pleased to be able to give Joe something he could take to her and maybe gain a few extra brownie points at the same time.

$\mathcal{I}$ still have plenty of days when I need to pinch myself. It can be hard to take in the fact that I work in one of the most stunningly beautiful houses in England, especially as it's a common occurrence for me to sit chatting with the Duke or Duchess of Ravensbury. Today was one of those days. I had a meeting with the Duchess to discuss the catering for a private event she was hosting, and so here I was, on a seemingly ordinary Thursday morning, looking out of the window of the private study she shared with her husband.

The Duchess is a handsome woman; slim, but not waiflike. There is a physical strength in her posture and figure that is matched by a determination and focus in her eyes. The expression 'eyes in the back of their head' seems to have been invented for her, yet she doesn't instil a sense of fear. Instead, she inspires great loyalty, and I have never heard a single negative word directed towards the Duchess. People find her impressive and warm. She loves Charleton House and talks about that love openly. Fascinated by the history of the family she has married into, she doesn't shy away from discussing the more colourful Fitzwilliam-Scott characters and their exploits. The Duke has the same attitude; there are no skeletons in their closets, the Duke having long since invited them all to dinner.

The only thing about the Duchess that's difficult to fathom is her dislike of coffee. She hates the stuff, an attitude I find impossible to relate to.

'It's not the most spectacular of views,' the Duchess said as she handed me a delicate china cup of coffee and glanced out of the window, 'but as the courtyard below is off limits to the public, it does make for a quiet working life.' Outside were brightly coloured window boxes along the sills of all the lower windows, and Robin was currently replanting a number of them. Beyond that, it was a simple, small stone courtyard that I wasn't aware served any particular purpose; at least, not anymore.

The Duchess took a seat behind an enormous wooden desk that would have needed an army of men to move. I guessed everything stayed where it was in this room; no spur of the moment furniture rearranging, and if it wasn't feng shui, then so be it. A second desk, the Duke's, sat at a right angle to the Duchess's. Against the other two walls were waist-high bookcases and a couple of ancient wooden filing cabinets, which I imagined getting stuck on a regular basis and requiring a lot of cursing and shoving to open. Although bearing in mind this was the office of a duke and duchess, the likelihood was the furniture behaved as well as the staff did when they were nearby.

Dozens of photos in exquisite silver frames lined the tops of bookcases and the walls were home to portraits, both painted and photographed, of family members and friends. Photos of presidents and prime ministers being welcomed to the house were interspersed with group photos of university students: a much younger Duke stood among his mainly male classmates, all in bow ties and tails at Oxford University. Privilege and confidence oozed from every pore.

I spotted Malcolm; even in a black-and-white photo, it was possible to make out his ruddy cheeks. In his youth, he'd had a sturdier build than all the others. He looked as if he would have been the life and soul of the party, always inviting people – friends and strangers alike – back to his rooms. It was likely, of course, that he would have done that to fit in with a class of people very different to his own.

Recalling my reason for being there, I sat opposite the Duchess and opened my notebook. We were planning a simple afternoon tea for a group of women who were paying a lot of money to have a tour of some of the private areas of the house with the Duchess. I would make sure there was an almost endless supply of champagne, sandwiches with the crusts removed and cakes so delicately decorated, they would be worthy of going in a display case alongside works of art. Or at least, I knew that was what was expected of me and I would spend the next three weeks working with Ruth, practising until our knuckles cramped and we never wanted to ice another cake in our lives.

'I love the idea of gin and tonic cupcakes. Would you mind making me some for this weekend? I have a friend staying and I just know she'll adore them.'

I was pleased the Duchess was so taken with the idea. 'Absolutely, and if you have any particular requests for the other cakes, please let me know.'

The Duchess considered the question for a moment. 'I'll leave that in your hands, Sophie. I have quite a lot on and don't want to give this event any more thought than absolutely necessary.'

We both turned as the door opened to admit her husband. I stood.

'Good morning, Duke.'

'Sit, please, none of that. I just need to collect some papers off my desk. How are you, Sophie?'

'Well, thank you.' When I had first met the Duke and Duchess, I had referred to them by the appropriate address of 'Your Grace' and 'Ma'am', but Mark had quickly put me right. He told me that they were a little more laid back than that, and insisted that staff simply call them Duke or Duchess. It had made me feel part of the 'inner sanctum'.

'Where did I put the damned thing?' As he rooted through a mound of paper on his untidy desk, the Duchess and I finalised a few more aspects of afternoon tea: which kinds of tea would be served; how many choices of coffee; different milk options. We really were catering to all potential requirements.

'Got it.' The Duke interrupted our conversation. 'I swear I'd lose my head if it wasn't screwed on. Sophie, you often have your ear to the ground. Any updates on the murder of that poor man?' He perched on the edge of his desk and turned to face me.

'Nothing substantial that I'm aware of. A lot of dead ends and anyone of interest has an alibi, but I know that DC Greene and his colleagues are working extremely hard.'

'Oh absolutely, I wouldn't suggest otherwise, but I do hate loose ends and we'd all like to move on.'

I was confused. 'I saw you with DI Flynn at the reception on the night of the theft. Hasn't he been keeping you up to date with events?'

The Duke smiled. 'Ah yes, your friend the detective inspector. Seems to think that any assistance you gave his team in the past was unnecessary, and feels the same way about current or future cases.'

I glanced down at my hands – was this a warning?

'Of course, my view is that if anything you did helped speed things along, then you were clearly essential, and I for one don't have an issue with that. Not that I'd say that to the inspector.' He had an impish smile on his face. Every time I met the Duke, he gave me another reason to like him. As he seemed talkative and supportive of my curious nature, I took the chance to question him.

'Is there any more news about your mother's bowl?'

He sighed deeply. 'None. My greatest frustration is that it is of absolutely no value to anyone else, so there is no gain from the theft, just the great sense of loss that is left behind. It's utterly pointless.'

'So it had to be an opportunist. If anyone knew of its lack of value, they wouldn't have bothered taking it, I presume?'

I'd meant that to be more rhetorical than it had sounded and I wasn't sure I'd meant to say it out loud, but the Duke took hold of my thoughts.

'Are you saying that if there was a chance it was chosen intentionally, then it must have been taken by someone who knew its loss would cause emotional distress?'

I hadn't actually been saying that; I hadn't even thought it, but he was onto something and I wanted to build on it.

'Who knows how much it means to you? I mean, visitors see it all the time and know the history, but don't necessarily know the sentimental value attached to it.'

'Only the family, I think. Of course, I often talk fondly of my mother, and there are a lot of items in the house that you could assume I attached a sentimental value to, but I can't see why anyone other than family would be aware of the additional significance of this piece. I've been in touch with various friends in the antiques business and they're all on the lookout for it. If anyone tries to sell it to a respected dealer, we'll know about it, so I guess I just have to play a waiting game. Well, on that slightly sombre note, I must be off.'

As he reached the door, he paused and looked over at his wife.

'Don't forget, we're meeting Jeremy and Belinda for cocktails at four. Are you planning on wearing the blue number I saw hanging on the back of the door?'

'I am.' The Duchess sounded a little uncertain, as though she expected him to say he didn't like the dress.

'Good.' He smiled and winked at her before heading out of the door. The Duchess laughed and looked at me.

'He can be such a lad sometimes.' She paused before adding, 'I'm very lucky.'

. . .

I left the Duchess to her work and thoughts of her young-at-heart husband, keen to talk to Robin, who was still working in the courtyard below. My route took me down a short, narrow staircase with whitewashed walls and plain wooden steps. In the past, it would have been used by servants making their way to their quarters at the end of a long working day.

I appeared from behind a hidden door at the top of an enormous, imposing oak staircase. Every inch of the walls was covered with muskets, bayonets, pistols, swords, daggers and body armour. Early generations of the Fitzwilliam-Scott family had fought for King and Country, this magnificent display a reminder of their role in bloody battles and the fight to win the approval of reigning monarchs. The weapons had been hung like works of art: concentric circles of swords and daggers formed a starburst around a silver chest plate; the crossed muzzles of muskets made blocks of patterns. I briefly considered how the tools of war could be used to create something so beautiful as I passed visitors reading guidebooks or listening intently to their audio guides, and those who were experiencing the house entirely from behind the lens of their camera-phone.

I quickly stepped out of the way as a visitor walked into the centre of the staircase without looking in order to take a selfie. Touching her arm gently, I drew her attention to how close she was to the edge of the step and she smiled gratefully. I didn't want any Darwin Awards handed out to visitors of Charleton House; not today, anyway.

I found the window that Robin had used to access the courtyard and, in a very unladylike fashion, clambered out to join him.

'Sophie, let me give you a hand.' I already had two feet on the ground by the time he reached me. 'What on earth are you doin'?'

'I wanted a quick word with you, do you have a minute?'

'Of course, let's sit over here in the sunlight. What's so important that you're prepared to climb through windows to see me? I'd be flattered, but I'm a little old to be your type.'

I'd warmed to Robin as soon as I'd met him last summer. He had a slightly old-fashioned way about him, but he was never offensive; more of a gentleman with a cheeky wit.

'I wanted to ask you about Saturday morning, if you don't mind. I know the police have spoken to you, but I just want to get something straight in my mind.'

'Get somethin' straight in your mind? Are you moonlighting for the police now? Cupcakes and crime, that's quite a mix.'

'I know. Technically it's none of my business. I can't quite explain why I'm so interested, but I have so many snippets of information coming my way that they end up swimming about my head and I need to make sense of them. It's a bit like someone has put a load of ingredients down in front of me; I can't help but wonder what I could make with them, what they'll look like once I've worked out quantities and what order they should be added into the mix.'

I'd never thought of my interest in Ben's murder in this way before. Sitting in the quiet courtyard with nothing to disturb me but the seemingly genuine interest of a sweet man like Robin made it easier for me to throw some light on why I was digging into motives and alibis; why I was so determined to find out what had happened. My mind instinctively wanted to piece things together, only this time it was a murder, not a meringue or a muffin.

'You said that on the morning of the murder, you were working with Elliot?'

'That's right, we were up near the Rock Garden. I knew the night before that we were on top of everything for the festival, so I'd scheduled in some other jobs for the team until about 9am when we knew the stallholders would start arriving so we needed to be back by the Great Pond and available to help them.

Elliot's rather fond of the Rock Garden so I had him up there with me.'

'You were up there all morning?'

'Let me think. I have it all on a spreadsheet back at the office, but off the top of my head, we started work at six. A number of us were in the greenhouses until seven, and then Elliot and I went up to the Rock Garden. We were there until eight-thirty, we grabbed a quick coffee together back in the break room, and then we both made our way over to the stalls to start helping there.' He laughed. 'You don't think I did it, do you?'

I smiled and nudged him with my elbow. 'Even weeds get handled gently by you, so I doubt it. Look, this is a bit awkward, but how well do you know Elliot?'

He looked at me with one raised eyebrow. 'Really? You think he did it?'

'I'm not saying that. It's just... well, did you see him flip out at Ben on Friday when they were setting up? Elliot was really mad, I thought he was going to hit Ben.'

Robin shook his head. 'I didn't see it, but I heard about it. Elliot can get a bit hot-headed; people often describe him as someone who shouldn't be crossed, but he's the kind of person that explodes and then comes back down to earth almost as quickly. I've never known him actually hit someone.'

I found that hard to believe; I'd never seen someone have to rein themselves in quite so much. Elliot had been as mad as hell.

'Can you think back to Saturday morning? Are you sure that Elliot was with you the whole time you were up at the Rock Garden? Was he ever out of your sight, no matter for how short a period of time?'

Robin rubbed his soil-covered hands across his face, leaving a brown streak on one of his cheeks. 'You're barking up the wrong tree, Sophie, honestly, love. Like I told the police, I was with him the whole time. We were tidying up the borders, making notes of what areas might need refreshing, picking up some rubbish, then I had to…'

He stopped and thought for a moment.

'Hang on, there was a point where… oh God, I forgot all about it. I didn't mention it to the police.'

'What?'

'Look, I still don't think for one minute that Elliot had anything to do with Ben's murder, but there was a point when I left him to it. You know the old shepherd's hut on the path that leads to the Rock Garden? We used to use it to sell ice cream in the summer, and then your predecessor decided it wasn't profitable enough. Well I'd noticed on the way past that a couple of the panes of glass in the small windows had been broken, so I went in to tidy them up and put a couple of pieces of cardboard in the holes, make them safe. I must have been in there twenty, maybe thirty minutes at the most. When I got back, Elliot was right where I had left him.

'He's a good man, Sophie. Hot-headed, yes, but he's a kind, reliable man who dotes on his family and loves his job. He wouldn't jeopardise that, no matter what it was that Ben had done to make him so angry.'

There was a pleading look in Robin's eyes. I liked him a lot, and I trusted him. But I didn't know Elliot, and I certainly had no idea if he could be trusted.

CHAPTER 13

*L*eaving Robin looking pensive, I felt bad for spoiling his day like that, but at least I had jogged his memory. I knew how easy it was for things to be so routine or instinctive that they didn't stand out in your mind, so I didn't blame him for not remembering that bit of information when he had been questioned by the police. No wonder detectives on police shows always handed out their card and said, 'Call me if you think of anything else.'

I didn't have any more meetings until after lunch, so decided to check out the Rock Garden. The glaring summer sun was still hanging around, but it was a little chillier than it had been at the weekend, and every time I walked into shadows, I shivered. The Rock Garden was about fifteen minutes' walk from the house if you knew where you were going, but I wanted to be sure.

Most visitors stumbled upon the Rock Garden accidentally as it was tucked away behind a small thicket of trees, and the pathways that brought you to it were winding and branched off in different directions at numerous junctions, but you were in for a treat when you made it. A waterfall tumbled over a mountain of dark grey rocks, then down a steep bank, round a few twists and turns, and finally into a large rocky pond. A maze of paths mean-dered their way up and down the surrounding ground, past rocks and displays of beautiful flowers.

I recognised a swathe of purple as a bank of irises. Pretty little violet-blue flowers covered the ground immediately next to the water, and the colour theme continued with deep purple flowers that had round pin cushion-like heads on tall green stalks. I was determined to learn more about horticulture now I was here and I made a mental note to ask Robin to walk me round this area and teach me a few things.

There were some visitors around, stopping to bend over and smell the flowers, or read the miniature wooden signs that said what they were. An elderly couple sat on a bench opposite the pond, holding hands as they took in their surroundings, occa-sionally following the flight path of a bird or pointing something out to one another. It seemed like everyone who walked these paths found themselves afraid to disturb the sounds of nature, opting to whisper to their companions if they deemed any conversation necessary.

I checked my watch; it was two thirty-two. Setting off down the path at a decent pace, round the pond, back up the other side of the waterfall, around the trees, over a miniature meadow and along a gravel path, I had a few more twists and turns and two gates to walk through. Once I made it to roughly where Silver Bullet Coffee had been based on Saturday morning, I checked my watch. It had taken me nine minutes. Bearing in mind that I didn't know any short cuts, I wasn't wearing the right footwear for cutting across flowerbeds, and I had walked at a steady but not particularly fast pace, I figured that Elliot could have made it in six or seven minutes. That gave him time to have a ten-minute argument with Ben, kill him and make it back to the Rock Garden in time for Robin to find him at work. OK, so it was cutting it fine, I knew that, but it was possible. If Elliot was already in a bad mood and had been quietly fuming all morning over whatever Ben had said and done, then it wouldn't have taken long for him to get mad enough to kill him. I couldn't explain how Elliot would have known Ben was alone in the van, but maybe he didn't. Maybe he just took a chance and got lucky. Either way, Elliot had the opportunity to kill Ben. Now I just needed to find out if he had a motive strong enough to kill someone.

Behind Charleton House, just beyond the back lane, is an enormous yard that's home to the gardens team. Five huge greenhouses stand side by side; surrounding these are old single-storey stone buildings, and every corner of the yard is dedicated to something: oversized plant pots; trees waiting to go into the gardens; a miniature allotment; small electric-powered vehicles; free-standing signage waiting to be called into use. It looks like well-organised chaos; it is busy and definitely lacks space.

I walked past the greenhouses, peering in as I went by. A number of them were empty, but in some there were signs that the team was starting to prepare the winter bedding plants. Small plant pots stood in hundreds of rows, some containing fresh soil, others waiting to be filled.

A black and white cat trotted past me, then backtracked and rubbed itself around my ankles before disappearing into another greenhouse. I spotted a cat bed and bag of dried cat food in the corner and guessed it was a stray who had been made welcome and, if it was anything like Pumpkin, now ran the show.

I spotted Elliot ahead of me, sitting on a low red-brick wall, cleaning tools. He was using a wire brush to scrub off the worst of the muck and had a focused look on his face.

'Elliot?'

He looked up. 'Yes?'

'I'm Sophie, we've not met before. I run the cafés.'

He nodded and turned back to the tools. 'What can I do for you?'

'This will sound a bit odd, but I wanted to ask you about Ben, the man who was killed.'

Elliot immediately stiffened and stopped what he was doing, but he didn't look at me.

'I know you knew him and I thought maybe you could tell me about him.'

'I've nuthin' to say.'

'So you did know him?'

'I told you, I've nuthin' to say.' Elliot started cleaning the tool again, only this time with even more vigour. It was only at that point that I noticed the size of the blade on the large pair of shears he had in his hands.

'Elliot, I saw the way you spoke to him on Friday. A lot of people did...'

'I've already spoken to the police, it's none of your business.'

'You nearly broke my arm when you slammed into me as you walked towards him. The resultant bruise rather makes it my business.'

Elliot stood. As much as I'm used to being the smallest person in the room, having him stand over me with a large, sharp blade in his hands made him seem about ten feet tall. I slightly regretted being so brusque with him, but I didn't warm to the silent, moody type at the best of times, and he was being foolish if he didn't think people were going to be interested in him after his display of anger towards Ben.

'It's none of your damned business.' He scooped up a couple more tools and marched off across the yard. I followed close on his heels.

'Elliot, I'm not saying you're involved, I just want to know if there's anything you can tell me that will help. I'm trying to figure out what happened.'

'What the hell has it got to do with you anyway?' He didn't wait for an answer and strode through a large open door into one of the stone buildings. Hanging in perfect order along the back wall were dozens of tools: hoes, shears, scissors, knives, shovels – you name it. They were spotless and clearly cared for; many of them also looked extremely sharp and I started to regret following him in.

Elliot hung up the tools he had been cleaning, and then turned to face me. 'Back off, I'm warning you.' His eyes were wide and there was a fury in them as he stormed past me, bashing into me as he went. 'Oh, I'm sorry,' he shouted sarcastically over his shoulder.

I was relieved that he'd gone. I knew there were cameras in the yard, but I still didn't feel safe around him, no matter what Robin had said about his temper flaring up but crashing down just as quickly.

I watched Elliot walk into the gardeners' break room. It was three o'clock and the first shift would be clocking off now. A number of gardeners were already leaving for the day, bags over their shoulders, striding towards freedom and a chance to rest their weary bodies. I left them to it and walked back towards the lane, wondering how on earth I was going to find out what Ben and Elliot had been arguing about.

It turned out that Elliot had taken a different route to the lane, and by the time I arrived, he was already standing by the security gate, chatting to one of the guards and looking a lot calmer. I hovered in the background and watched as a small car pulled up next to him. Elliot drew his conversation to a close as a woman with long blonde hair tied back in a ponytail got out and walked over to him. They briefly kissed, and after she'd exchanged a few words with the guard, they both got in the car. She performed a nifty three-point turn, and as they drove off, Elliot stuck his arm out of the window and waved at the guard. A small child I hadn't noticed before did the same thing, its arm barely visible from within the child seat.

'Sophie?' The car had just driven past Joyce and she was heading my way. 'Are you alright? You look miles away, have you been neglecting to top up your caffeine levels? Nice top – I keep telling you that brighter colours suit you, and I'm glad to see you're listening.'

'Hmm?' I looked down to see what she was talking about. I'd gone for a loose-fitting wide-necked t-shirt that was bright red on one side and navy blue on the other. Bold, but still smart enough to wear when meeting the Duchess.

'Now, if I were you, I'd finish it off with an extremely chunky necklace, either bright red or navy. A pair of bright red shoes would be perfect and... ooh, you ought to get yourself some glasses with a red frame. Daring, but with your silver hair you could pull it off. You'd look marvellous.'

Once I assumed that my fashion consultation was over, I changed the subject. 'What do you know about Elliot?'

'Forrester? Been here for years, wouldn't surprise me if he came here straight from school. Never quite become one of the old guard, though. Not old enough for a start, but he's also a bit aloof, hard to warm to. You've heard about the girlfriend, right?'

I shook my head.

'Well, a few years ago...' Joyce linked her arm through mine and steered me towards the side door that would take us to the Library Café. I mentally checked that I had some decent cake to offer her, and then tuned back into what she was saying.

'...Carla had only been here about a month...'

'Hang on, who's Carla?'

'Pay attention, girl! The woman in the car, Elliot's girlfriend. I'll start again. Carla started working as a gardener here a few years back and had only been here a month or so when she and Elliot got together. Love's young dream, they were. We were quite relieved; Elliot had always been a bit sour faced, but he seemed to perk up when she arrived. We actually started to see him smile – personally I thought his face was going to crack. Well, they were together about six months when things seemed to get a bit rocky. Elliot's period of smiling was over and she got a bit withdrawn.'

We'd reached the café and I got Joyce to take a break and grab us a table. There was plenty of choice as the visitors were starting to thin out. I cut a couple of slices of lemon drizzle cake, made two mugs of coffee and returned to join her. The enormous chunk of cake that Joyce indelicately shovelled into her mouth kept her quiet for a minute, and I took the time to admire today's choice of nail polish. She had opted for a delicate pale pink, but each nail had the added detail of a small – I presume fake – diamond. I just hoped one didn't come off and get swallowed up with the cake. Joyce wasn't the most delicate woman I'd come across, but she was inhaling the cake like she hadn't eaten for a week.

She paused and looked at me, at the plate, then at the full slice of cake I was holding, and smiled coyly. 'It's been a busy day, I barely had time for lunch.'

'But you did have time for it?'

'Well, yes, but… oh, be quiet. Are you going to eat that?'

I quickly took an enormous bite of my own slice and grinned at her triumphantly as crumbs fell from the corners of my mouth onto the table. Joyce laughed and I covered my mouth with my hand to avoid hitting her with crumbs as I joined in. Some people found Joyce intimidating, but I found myself able to relax easily around her, and I loved her upfront nature.

Once I'd swallowed my mouthful, I got her back on track. 'You were saying something about a rocky patch between Carla and Elliot.'

'Ah yes. Well, we all thought that things were going to be short-lived – this was just six months after they'd started dating. Neither of them looked happy, and then all of a sudden, she left. No one knew why – here one minute, gone the next.

'Things got back to normal and no one talked about it anymore. Elliot was back to sulking around the place, and then three months later, he perked up again. We started to wonder if he was dating someone else, but no, it turned out that he and Carla had never actually split up and he was grinning like the Cheshire Cat because she was pregnant.'

I tried to do the maths. 'What are we talking here? Two, three years ago?'

Joyce paused, the mug just in front of her lips, the jewels glinting on her impossibly long nails.

'Little Isabella was born three years ago, so Carla must have started a year or two before that.'

'You made it sound like there was something scandalous. That just sounds like normal relationship ups and downs, with a baby thrown in, albeit quite quickly.'

Joyce waved a glittery nail in my direction. 'Hold your horses. When Isabella was about three months old, a rumour started going round my team. Heaven knows how they got hold of it, but once I got wind of it, I gave them all a lecture on spreading gossip and the damage it can do. I wasn't specific, of course, but they must have known what I was talking about. That put an immediate stop to it.'

I wasn't surprised – Joyce had instilled the fear of God in her team. They loved her and were terrified of her in equal parts.

'They were saying that the baby wasn't Elliot's and Carla had stopped working here because she'd had an affair with someone. He'd forgiven her on the understanding that she quit her job and stay away from "him", whoever "he" was.'

'So she'd slept with someone they worked with?'

'That was the assumption.' Joyce didn't sound in the slightest bit judgmental, but that didn't surprise me. I knew that she had, until recently, been 'the other woman' in a relationship. 'We never found out who it was; there's always some turnover in the gardens team, so he might still be working here, he might not. After a while it became yesterday's news. We often see Carla picking Elliot up from work and they seem happy enough. He dotes on Isabella, that's for sure; he's still a miserable devil, but not when his little girl is around.'

Joyce changed the subject, her story at an end. 'Now, tell me, when are you going to let me take you shopping?'

I smiled as the image of flying pigs appeared in my mind.

CHAPTER 14

There was a knock at the door. I knew it was Mark so I called out that it was open.

'It's just me, I come bearing gifts. Bloody hell, what's that?'

I dropped my knife and walked out into the hallway. Mark and Pumpkin were standing stock still opposite each other. They'd never got on.

'That's Pumpkin. You met her the last time you were here, and the time before that.'

'I know, but she wasn't this big last time, was she? I think Pumpkin's eaten a pumpkin. A large one. More than one.'

'Oi, you're talking about a family member, and you're on her home turf, so be nice.'

'I will, I will, for fear she'll eat me if I don't.' He tentatively stepped past her. She gave him a look that made it very clear she still wasn't warming to him.

Once we were back in the kitchen, I put my hand out. 'Come on, then, where's this gift?'

He handed me a narrow paper bag with string handles. 'You might have already bought it for yourself, but if so, I doubt you'll mind having two.'

I reached in and pulled out a bottle of Twenty Trees Gin. The small distiller – and by small, I mean one man and a garden shed – had been at the food festival and I'd had a taste. It was delicious. Mark was right, I had bought myself a bottle, but I was so impressed that I was very happy to have a second ready and waiting.

I handed him a couple of glass tumblers and the bottle I'd already opened. Setting him to making us both drinks, I returned to preparing a salad and the swordfish steaks I was going to serve. After we'd raised a toast to gin distillers everywhere, Mark sat at the table and watched me chop a multi-coloured array of tomatoes.

'Nice job above the fireplace. Have you ever thought about moonlighting as an interior designer?' From where he was, Mark could see into the sitting room and he'd spotted the four splotches of paint on the chimney breast. I'd moved in twelve months ago and had been slow at making my mark on the place.

'I know, I know, I just can't decide.'

'Between white, white, white or white? Tough choice.' He had a thoughtful look on his face, but I knew he was teasing.

'Get up close and they're very different. I want the room to feel bathed in light, but not too sterile.' I handed him a pencil. 'Go and rank them, I'm sure you have an opinion.' He went through and stared intently at the wall while we continued our conversation through the doorway.

'I saw you sniffing around the gardeners' yard today, do you have any updates for me?' he asked as he wrote on the wall.

'Not really, but I have a question. Were you aware of the rumour about Elliot's girlfriend having an affair?'

He nodded. 'Most people were, but it's old news.'

'Any idea who she slept with?'

'Not a clue, and it was probably better that no one found out. I'm sure we'd have had a murder on our hands a couple of years ago if that had got out. Why?' Mark returned and sat back at the table, the pencil tucked behind his ear.

'I'm trying to find things that link back to Ben. Guy, Kyle and Elliot are the most closely associated with him, plus they all had a good idea of where he would be on Saturday morning. Kyle is the first one I'm inclined to rule out. When I spoke to him after Ben was found dead, he seemed genuinely shocked and upset. I really don't think it was him, although his alibi is a bit shaky.

'Guy has Malcolm as an alibi and the time he signed in at reception matches his story. They were discussing a restaurant project in Paris, although Malcolm seemed a bit cagey about it, and I'm not sure I'd want advice from Guy. If Guy's involved with, or even just supportive of a company rebranding someone else's product as their own, then he's not a very ethical business-man. Who knows what he gets up to in London? I know for sure I wouldn't want to eat at any restaurant he was involved with.

'There's the dodgy business with the coffee which could be behind this, but as far as we know, Ben might have supported the whole thing. It might even have been his idea, so I don't think he was killed because he was against them doing that. Elliot, on the other hand, had the opportunity, and he clearly had an issue with Ben, but we don't know any details. Then, of course, there's Bruce Keen. If he has found out what the Silver Bullet lads were up to, then he's certainly got a motive; I just don't know if it's enough to make him want to kill someone over it.'

'Did Bruce have the opportunity?' Mark asked.

'Possibly. He was at the festival that morning to meet me, but I have no idea what time he arrived. He has enough contacts among the stallholders for someone to have signed him in as one of their team. There's often a change in staffing at the last minute, so sometimes our security staff are told how many people are coming from one organisation, but not given their names. It's not great and the security team shouldn't be doing it, but it's the reality. He's also been taking a lot of interest to how the investigation is going. When he came to drop off some samples, it was all he would talk about. It's all just swimming around in my head.'

'You do realise...' Mark let his thought hang temptingly in the air for a moment. 'If Elliot was out of Robin's sight for thirty minutes or so, then no one saw Robin either. His alibi has just gone to pot.'

I'd already thought of that. 'True, but I checked the shepherd's hut and you can see where he's repaired the windows. He's in the clear.'

'Oh.' Mark looked deflated. 'I've no idea then. I need food. Maybe then I'll be able to think straight' – he smirked – 'although that would be a first.'

We spent the rest of the evening discussing Bill and Mark's ongoing debate about where they were next going on holiday and who we should attempt to set Joyce up with. Neither topic reached any conclusion. At one point Pumpkin wandered into the room, hoping for a chunk of swordfish. I'd already saved her a big piece and put it on a saucer for her. Once she had finished trying to lick the enamel off the plate and was satisfied there wasn't even so much as a sniff of fish left, she leapt from floor to window ledge to the top of the fridge and took a bath while keeping half an eye on us.

Mark was impressed. 'I would have thought she'd need a hydraulic lift to make it up there.'

I offered Mark coffee.

'Aren't you missing something?' I looked at him blankly. 'There's no dessert?' He looked genuinely horrified. It had completely slipped my mind, but then I had spent all day feeding him cakes, pastries and any other sweet goods that didn't make it from the oven to the display cases fast enough to avoid his gaze. I could have argued, but his desire for 'something naughty' was stronger than any argument I could present.

'Get your coat,' I ordered him.

'What? I only asked where dessert was, you don't have to kick me out.'

'Get your coat, we're going over the road. I'll buy you one of those crème brûlées you love so much.'

Despite it being a warm evening, we opted to stay inside at the Black Swan. We grabbed the seat in the large window that overlooked the beer garden and I went to order a crème brûlée and a glass of white port for Mark – I figured that the port would make up for me neglecting to make dessert. For myself, I opted for summer berry pudding and a decaf coffee.

As I returned to our seats, Mark pointed in the direction of the beer garden. I followed the line of his finger and saw Guy sitting on his own under a large umbrella. His attention was focused on his phone.

'Inevitable, I suppose, he is staying here.'

'Why is that?' asked Mark. 'If Silver Bullet is a local company, why didn't he go home once the festival finished?'

'The company is local, but he's not. He lives in London and leaves Kyle and Ben – well, Kyle now – to manage things here. He seems to come along for the fun stuff. The police told him he had to stay around.'

Our desserts and drinks arrived and Mark tucked in. Between each bite, he cleaned the spoon as thoroughly as Pumpkin had cleaned her saucer. He didn't speak until his dish was empty.

'That filled the spot, thank you. Chin-chin.' He clinked his glass against my coffee cup. I was about to ask him if he had a busy day tomorrow when his eyes swivelled from one side of the room to the other. I turned to see what had caught his attention.

'Don't look,' he hissed. 'Wait, I don't want them to know I've spotted them.' He'd dropped a little lower in his seat, using my head as something to hide behind.

'Oh for heaven's sake, it's a pub. Everyone is always checking out everyone else, especially the locals, and I like to consider myself a local now.'

I turned to see the back of Guy's head at the bar. He was handed two pints, one of which he passed to a man standing next to him. Then he led the way through the door that accessed the bedrooms.

I turned back to Mark. 'Do you recognise him?'

'No, never seen him before, but they're pretty pally. I watched him arrive. They had one of those man hugs – you know, lots of back slapping but keeping about an inch apart, just in case someone should think they're anything other than men's men who do manly things and love the ladies.'

I laughed at his description; I knew exactly what he meant.

'Wait here, I might be able to find out.' Mark drained what was left of his port and got up. I watched him out of the window as he walked down the centre of the garden and through a wooden gate. From where I sat, I could just see the corner of the car park and the first four spaces. One of them was filled by a racing green Jaguar, and Mark slowly circled it. He nodded a few times and scratched his chin, to all intents and purposes looking like a car buff who was impressed with what he saw. In reality, I didn't know anyone less interested in cars, but he was doing a fine job of looking otherwise. He got closer and peered in through a window, then moved to the rear window and did the same. Finally, he stepped back, gave another nod of approval, then sauntered down the path and back into the pub.

'You're a natural.'

'What?' It came out as a grunt as he landed on the seat.

'You looked like a true petrol-head.'

'Ha, it's all these years of pretending that my tour groups have just asked the most interesting questions I've ever heard. It hones my acting skills. Now, do you want to know who Guy's pal is or not?'

'You know?'

He looked very pleased with himself. 'There's a stack of paperwork on the back seat and a couple of his business cards are scattered on the passenger seat. Guy is currently meeting with Chester Manning, an antiques dealer from Buxton, specialising in rare antiquities.' He folded his arms and sat back. 'You, my darling girl, owe me a drink.'

CHAPTER 15

Despite the events of last night, and the gin and tonic I'd eventually succumbed to at the pub, I'd managed to get a decent night's sleep, which was a good thing; the cafés were packed. The continuing good weather was bringing people to Charleton House in their droves, and no matter how warm it got, they still wanted a cup of hot tea or coffee.

I started by helping the Stables Café team set up, leaving them to it as they were swamped by a group of dog walkers who had started their day early. Then I hot-footed it back to a meeting in the Garden Café, where I reprimanded a couple of staff members for the scruffy state of their shoes. In the Library Café, I threw half a dozen trays of pastries in the oven, prepared what felt like hundreds of single-serve quiches, and then gave the team a hand clearing tables. I was hot and sweaty, but happy. This was one of the many reasons I loved my job. I couldn't spend all day in an office or in meetings, or I'd go crazy. Nor could I spend all day on my feet in a café, but combine all these things and I was in my element.

I was carrying a tray piled high with dirty dishes when Mark appeared. He was followed by a group of about ten elderly women, covered head to toe in floral prints, and every one was wearing straw hats with purple ribbons around them.

'Well, girls,' he called out across the group, 'I must say goodbye to you, but as promised, I am leaving you with easy access to tea and cake.'

The women oohed and aahed with relief.

'I can highly recommend the chocolate croissants, and they do a mean lemon drizzle cake here. There's a large table in the corner that's free, so why don't you make yourselves comfortable and I'll arrange for someone to come and take your order.'

As a rule we didn't do table service in the Library Café, but we sometimes made an exception if Mark appeared with a group that he had clearly become fond of and wanted to go the extra mile for. I fetched a staff member and sent them over to the table.

Once Mark had freed himself from the overly eager octogenarians, he walked over to me and dramatically leant on my shoulder.

'They are adorable, every one of the old dears, but I am exhausted. I haven't been drilled so thoroughly or laughed so hard in years.'

'I'll refuel you, don't worry. Go and say goodbye to your fan club and I'll prepare your favourites.'

I watched as Mark returned to his group. All eyes were on him as the women thanked him and told him how wonderful he'd been. His hands were clasped, his arm held firmly, and he was kissed until his cheeks were covered in bright pink lipstick. They all insisted on photos being taken, and after he'd fought off their attempts to give him tips – and no doubt a few offers to take him home – he was released and joined me at a small table on the far side of the room. I handed him a napkin and he discreetly wiped the lipstick kisses from his face.

I laughed. 'That's a very eager fan club.'

'Bright as a button, every one of them. I almost feel sorry for their husbands.'

'Or wives,' I added.

'Of course, one shouldn't assume, although based on their fawning over me, I doubt it. I don't know what it is about little old ladies, they're like moths to a flamer.' He waited to see if I got the joke.

I groaned. 'That's dreadful.'

'But true. Now back to the most important business of the day – do you have a plan?' He sank his teeth into a chocolate croissant.

'Not really. I looked up Chester Manning on the internet when I got home. His website isn't very extensive, it just looks like your average antiques store. There are a few auctions coming up and there's a link to a very old newspaper interview he did, talking about French side tables from the eighteenth century, but nothing of any interest.'

'Nothing that links him and Guy?'

'Nothing at all.'

I waited while he gulped down half his mug of coffee in one go; I must have been staring.

'What? I've been talking non-stop all morning, I'm parched.'

I caught the eye of the team member who had just carried a tray of cakes over to Mark's group. 'Can you bring him another coffee? I'm concerned he's going to pass out if we don't get more fluid in him.'

The young woman looked at him; all my staff were used to Mark. 'You do realise coffee dehydrates?' she advised him, the smallest hint of humour detectable in her voice.

'You do realise I know your boss quite well and I'm sure she expects nothing but "yes sir, no sir" from all her staff?' he replied.

'Feel free to add pepper into his coffee, maybe some chilli powder.' I smirked at Mark as the grinning server walked off to the kitchen. 'I love my staff like you love your old ladies. Look, I don't have any meetings in my diary this afternoon, and I was thinking' – I scanned the room – 'this place could do with some antique French side tables. Maybe some lamps, perhaps even a couple more armchairs. It's a nice day out there, so we should go and browse some antiques. I've heard about a place in Buxton that might be worth checking out.'

'I couldn't think of anything I'd rather do. Why don't you collect me from my office when you're ready? I'm sure I'll have got my strength back by then.'

I decided that if the morning had been anything to go by, the Stables Café was going to be bursting at the seams come lunchtime, so once I'd packed Mark back to his office and arranged for his tour group to receive a discount on their bill, I set off up the back lane to help out. It was a challenge to walk along this short, private lane without being stopped multiple times by colleagues for a catch up, which was lovely, but meant I always needed to add at least ten minutes to any journey. Today was no exception, although I didn't mind too much. The Stables Café team wasn't actually expecting me; I would just be an extra pair of hands.

As I walked under the archway that led into the courtyard housing the café, I spotted a familiar face sitting at one of the outside tables. A young woman had a Jack Russell dog at her feet and a small child in a pushchair next to her. As I got closer, I recognised her as Carla – Elliot Forrester's girlfriend who had picked him up from work yesterday. I assumed the young girl was Isabella.

I looked around, but there was no sign of Elliot.

'Hi, Carla?'

'Yes?' She looked up from feeding the young girl carrot sticks, looking confused and clearly not recognising me. But then, why would she?

'I'm Sophie, I work here. I cross paths with the gardens team quite a lot, so I know Elliot.' I was stretching the truth so far it could snap at any point, but I needed her to relax. It seemed to work.

'Oh, hi. I don't think he's mentioned you, but I guess this place is so big.'

'It is. I've been here just over a year, but I still get lost on my way to meetings.'

Carla laughed. 'I know the feeling. I used to work here and I never went anywhere without a map. I thought I'd get my head around it, but I never did.'

'Do you miss it?'

Carla offered Isabella a small sandwich from a box she'd retrieved from under the pushchair.

'I do, but Elliot keeps me up to date on what's happening, and I still see old friends when I come and collect him.'

This was my chance. 'That must be nice. I've already made some great friends here. It's a wonderful community.' Carla nodded as I talked. 'You really see that at times like this – everyone's been so supportive.' I stopped and waited to see if she would react, but she didn't seem to pick up on what I was getting at, so I kept going. 'It was such a shock when that stallholder was murdered. Just awful, but everyone pulled together. Ben – that was his name. So sad.'

Carla went pale and stared down at her feet. She definitely knew him; there was no way she would have reacted like that if he had been a stranger.

'I'm sorry, was he a friend? I didn't mean to upset you. I didn't realise.'

'It's fine.' I waited for her to continue, but again she didn't say anything so I kept going.

'So many people have told me what a nice person he was. I only got to meet him briefly and he did seem really nice. No one's had a bad word to say about him.'

I watched as a smile started to form on her lips, but there was sadness in her eyes. 'He was very sweet.' She stroked Isabella's hair.

'So you knew him well?'

She nodded. 'Yes, I hadn't seen him much recently, but I used to know him.' Her gaze lingered on Isabella. The child was the classic blonde-haired blue-eyed cutie. It was easy to see why Elliot doted on her.

'Did Elliot know Ben?' I knew he had, but I wanted to give Carla a chance to explain before I bulldozed my way in. Her eyes dropped again; she started to pick at one of her fingernails.

'Sort of, but they weren't friends.'

'Did they not get on?'

She looked around the courtyard as though wanting to make sure she wasn't being watched. I assumed that she wanted to check Elliot wasn't around.

'Not really.' She stopped and I was sure that was as much as I was going to get. Carla didn't know me and she had no reason to tell me anything, but I was impatient.

'Carla, it's none of my business, but I know Elliot and Ben didn't get on. I witnessed Elliot laying into him the day before he was killed. He didn't hit him, but he looked like he really wanted to. This was in front of a lot of other people, so he didn't seem to care who was watching.'

'He didn't kill him, I swear!'

'I'm not saying he did, but what was he so angry about? Do you know?' Carla shook her head, but I knew she was lying. And I wasn't being entirely honest, either – Elliot was at the top of my suspect list. I just needed to understand why he'd wanted Ben dead.

As I watched Isabella eat a second little sandwich, I felt the cogs in my brain turn. Why on earth hadn't I realised it as soon as I'd heard the rumours about Carla's affair? Everyone thought that she'd slept with someone she worked with, but that was only hearsay. What if the affair part had been right, but the colleague part wrong? What if she'd had an affair with Ben, and Isabella was the outcome? What I didn't understand was why Elliot would want to kill Ben after all this time. Joyce had told me that Isabella was three years old now. Ben was local, and if Elliot was mad enough to want him dead, he'd had plenty of opportunity. Something must have set him off and triggered a renewed burst of fury, but what?

Carla looked at me. I knew she wanted me to leave well alone. Elliot clearly had a temper and I hoped that she was never on the receiving end of it, but there were no physical signs, and Joyce had talked about Elliot becoming happier again after Isabella's birth. Maybe fatherhood had calmed him down – with the exception of some recent Ben-related event.

'Sophie, sorry to disturb.' I looked away from Carla towards the member of staff who had come out to see me. 'We've got a customer who wants to talk to a manager and... well, I saw you out here. Would you mind?'

'Give me one minute.' The staff member walked away and I turned back to Carla. 'I'm just trying to understand why he was so cross. It might help.'

'It was nothing, I'm sure of it. You know what men can be like. They didn't see each other very often and Ben travelled a lot, so it was never a big deal that they just didn't get on.'

I knew I wasn't going to get anything else from her, and for her sake, I didn't want Elliot to find me questioning his girlfriend, so I said goodbye and went inside. Trying to figure out a murder was still new to me, but dealing with disgruntled customers – and I was sure that was going to be the case – was old hat. I took a deep breath and allowed a serene smile to spread across my face, determined to be the most charming version of myself. Kill 'em with kindness – it always worked.

In order to find Mark's office, it is necessary to step into the entrance lobby of one of the ladies' toilets that are available to the visitors. You then take a sharp right turn before venturing into the main area of the toilets – and if you are a man, being chased back out – and up a narrow flight of stairs marked 'Private'. Once you arrive, you find a large, bright and airy space that Mark shares with two others.

Despite the sharing aspect, Mark has still ended up with a space about four times the size of my office. Mind you, I wouldn't want to swap. The courtyard below is where school groups often gather and the noise is enough to prevent anyone from thinking. Then there is the occasional pipe blockage in the toilets below. The aroma when this happens is enough to force Mark and his colleagues out of their office and into the cafés to work. So, as much as I may be envious of the general airiness, that air could become the exact reason that I wouldn't want his office in a million years.

I knocked on the door frame and walked through the open door. Mark was chatting to a man wearing a long moss-green coat, matching breeches and cream stockings, sitting at the desk opposite him. His black shoes had a slight heel.

'Sophie, meet Lancelot Capability Brown. Ignore the smell, he's been dead for over two hundred years.'

Capability took his feet off the desk and stood. Removing his tri-cornered hat and revealing a grey wig with tight curls over the ears, he performed an exaggerated bow.

'Greetings. A pleasure to meet you.' He tossed the hat onto the desk and sat back down. 'Mark's just been filling me in on the adventure you have planned for this afternoon.' I scowled at Mark. We'd never actually said that we'd keep our activities quiet, but I had no idea who this man was or if he could be trusted.

Mark read my mind. 'It's fine, Capability and I go way back.'

'Besides which,' the man in the wig continued, 'I'm basically a ghost so no one will believe they've seen me, let alone what I've said.'

As I sat on the edge of a desk across the room from them both, I must have looked confused. Mark tried to clear things up for me.

'He's not actually a ghost, Sophie.' He threw a pen across the room and it hit the man in the chest. 'See? Solid.'

'Idiot,' was the only word I could think of to direct at my friend. I turned back to Capability. 'What are you up to today? Designing an addition to the garden?' As one of the country's most respected landscape architects of the eighteenth century, Lancelot 'Capability' Brown had worked at Charleton House and played a key role in the way the beautiful gardens looked today. I guessed he was going to be delivering a tour or performing somewhere outside, talking to visitors and telling them his story and plans in 'real time'.

'I'm thinking about a vine. We're possibly a little far north, but I've had great success installing a vine at Hampton Court Palace and I would like to try something similar here. Only instead of one large vine, I'm wondering about a small vineyard. I'm spending this afternoon considering the best location for it. There seem to be a lot of strange folk wandering around the garden in unusual garb and I'm finding their input most useful.'

'Give it a rest, Ed.' Mark sighed and stood up. 'Come on, Sherlock.'

I looked at Ed – or was it really Capability's ghost?

'Sorry to rush off, only I'm keen to follow up some information we found.'

'*I* found,' chipped in Mark, 'and I haven't forgotten that drink you owe me.'

We left the eighteenth-century gentleman at the computer, checking his emails. The longer I worked at Charleton House, the more I found my definition of 'odd' being redefined.

It was a thirty-minute drive to Chester Manning's antiques shop and we spent most of the journey going over what we knew about the various people in Ben's life. The good weather had yet to come to an end, the view across the Derbyshire hills was beautiful, and the further we went, the more I relaxed.

I drove us down a single-track lane that turned off the main road just as we hit the edge of Buxton. After waiting for a tractor to pass, I parked in front of a converted barn. The exterior wooden walls had been painted a gloss black, and with the burgundy red edging, it looked distinctly out of place. Far too grand and perfect for an old farm building. The sign for 'Manning Antiques' was just as showy. This wasn't going to be one of those places that looked like a junk shop and smelt of abandoned history and mothballs.

'So how are we going to play this?' Mark whispered as we walked in.

'We were passing and we're just browsing. Easy.'

'But exactly what are we looking for?'

'I have no idea. I guess we'll know it when we see it, or we'll just learn about his link with Guy. And before you ask, I have no idea how. Maybe it will come up in conversation.'

Mark didn't look at all convinced.

We stepped through the large double doors that were wedged wide open, and into the cold shadows of the barn. Just as I'd expected, the space was well laid out. The antiques had been displayed to resemble different rooms; it looked like a nineteenth-century IKEA store.

We wandered around a couple of the display rooms, running our hands over the furniture and making sounds of approval.

'Hmm, this is rather nice.'

'Superb quality, but not what we're looking for.'

'I'm sure my great-aunt Gertrude had a lamp just like this. Ah yes, this is hers. See that crack down the side? That's from the time she used it to hit my great-uncle after she discovered his affair with the scullery maid.'

Mark appeared to be relaxing into our charade and enjoying himself.

We wound our way through the leather armchairs and coffee tables. There was an enormous display of silverware and the collection of paintings seemed to exclusively depict scenes of Derbyshire. I couldn't imagine myself ever having any of the pieces in my own home, but there was no escaping the fact that Chester had taste and, judging by the price tags, his customers had the money to buy that taste.

'Can I help you?' I jumped as Chester appeared at my side. 'I'm so sorry, I didn't mean to startle you.'

I laughed awkwardly. 'It's fine. Err no, thank you. We were passing and thought we'd come and have a look. We're just browsing.'

'Well do shout if you need any assistance, I'm happy to help you with any spur-of-the-moment purchases.'

He smiled and made his way back to a desk just as the phone rang. I breathed a little more easily as his attention was focused on the caller. As he'd taken a seat and put his feet up on his desk, it looked as if it was going to be a long call. Or at least, I hoped so.

There was something familiar about him, and it wasn't just because I had seen him at the pub with Guy. Mind you, he wore the uniform of the upper class male and his outfit practically mirrored Malcolm's wardrobe: salmon pink trousers and a checked shirt. His brown leather belt was decorated with a weave of multi-coloured threads, he had the same ruddy complexion as Malcolm, and it was easy to imagine them sharing a sherry and discussing the stock market or how 'Tarquin was faring at Eton'.

I walked towards the back of the building and saw a couple of doors on the far wall. It seemed the building was actually split in two and there was a lot more that lay beyond the wall. I signalled to Mark and he made his way over to me.

'We need to go in there.'

'Why? What excuse are we going to give when he finds us rooting around?'

'We don't need an excuse. There are no "Staff only" or "Do not enter" signs; we'll say we just thought it was another area of the shop.'

'OK, you go in. It'll be obvious if we both suddenly disappear.'

He had a point. I checked that Chester was still distracted by the phone call and slipped in through one of the doors.

There were long shelves of vases, picture frames, snuff boxes – everything that you'd imagine looking at home in *Downton Abbey* could be found back here. Some items had tags on them that said 'reserved'; others looked as if they were waiting for a polish before they went out on display. The room was gloomy and I decided there was no way I was going to spot anything of any use, so I made my way back out into the showroom.

I caught Mark's eye and shook my head, pointing at the second door. He glanced at Chester and gave me the thumbs up.

This room was much brighter. There were large double doors pinned open on the far side, allowing the sunlight to come streaming in, but it was much less tidy than the first room I'd explored. A desk and a shelf full of files were in the far corner. An enormous table held remnants of bubble wrap and brown wrapping paper, and a pile of wooden crates was stacked up in the corner, waiting to be filled with delicate antiques and shipped out.

Next to the door was a stack of boxes, a couple of crates and some very well-padded envelopes. A look told me that they were all addressed, ready to go. As I took a step closer, I felt something crunch under my shoe, and then again under my other foot. I stepped back and looked down – whatever I had stood on was now brown powder.

There were more brown lumps scattered around. Stones? No, they were coffee beans. I picked one up and smelt it – I was right. I collected more until I had a handful of misshapen and small beans. There were a couple of Quakers: the under-ripe coffee seeds that had been picked too early. This wasn't good quality coffee; it hadn't been dried or milled carefully. This had been roasted by someone who was more interested in volume than quality – a company like the Northern Bean Company.

I followed a trail of beans on the floor and found more next to the large table. As I stood up to see if they were anywhere else, the name on one of the parcels caught my eye: 'Malcolm De Witt' and a Paris address. I took out my phone and snapped a picture of the box, grabbed a couple of the coffee beans and went to find Mark.

Mark was examining a painting close up – very close up. His nose was practically touching the canvas.

'Mark, look at this.' I opened up the photo on my phone, but he didn't turn towards me.

'No, look at this,' he said. 'I swear this farm hand looks just like you.'

'Mark, we don't have time. Stop it.'

I showed him the picture on the phone, but he wasn't impressed. 'So, Malcolm dropped by and did some shopping.'

'It's too much of a coincidence. Plus that box – it's the perfect size for the Duke's bowl. And I reckon the bowl would have been stored in a sack of coffee beans before it got here. *Silver Bullet* coffee beans.'

I gave Mark my best 'eureka' look. 'I still think she looks like you,' was his only response.

'Mark, for heaven's sake, take this seriously! I need you to stay here and make sure those parcels don't go anywhere. I'm going to call Joe and get him to meet you here.'

'And where are you going?'

'I need to have a chat with a certain coffee roaster. Also, I've remembered why Chester is so familiar looking. He went to university with both Malcolm and the Duke – all three of them are in a photo that's hanging in the Duke's office. None of this is a coincidence.'

Mark was paying attention now. 'How do I keep Chester occupied once he gets off the phone?'

'I have no idea. You could ask him for more information on that painting of me.'

I walked out of the barn as quickly as possible, nodding to Chester as I left. He gave a lazy wave – he could probably spot a time waster a mile off and I guessed he had put us in that category, so he was in no rush to get off the phone. I dialled Joe's number as I got in the car, then headed off to the pub.

CHAPTER 16

our o'clock in the afternoon wasn't, by my reckoning, too early for a gin and tonic, but that wasn't why I was pulling into the Black Swan car park. When I'd given Joe a rundown of what I had found at the antiques shop and made sure he was on his way there, I'd neglected to tell him where I was heading, but only because I couldn't be sure that I'd find who I was looking for. That, and Joe would tell me to mind my own business, and I didn't want him to spoil my fun. I felt like a hound who had got the scent and I didn't want to be dragged away from it.

As I turned the engine off and got out of the car, the back door of the pub opened and Kyle walked out with a large bag over his shoulder. Bingo!

'Hi, Sophie, day off?'

'No, I was looking for you. Do you have a minute?'

'Not really, I've just checked out and need to get on the road.' He hadn't actually stopped to talk to me. Putting his bag in the boot of the car and opening the driver's side door, the keys already in his hand, he seemed very keen to get going.

'I really need to have a word, Kyle, it's important.' I stared at him. He could run and there was no way I could stop him, but he looked tired, like a man who'd had enough. He stood for a moment, staring beyond me, and then sighed, closed the car door and finally returned my gaze.

'Can I buy you a drink?'

I nodded and let him lead the way back into the pub.

Kyle bought us a couple of cokes and we went outside to a table in the far corner of the garden where no one could overhear us. Running his finger round the rim of his glass, a haunting chime emanating from it as he did so, he again refused to look me in the eye.

'Kyle, I have a theory, and the police are on their way to check it out. A valuable item – sentimentally valuable, not financially valuable – was stolen from Charleton House a week ago. Right now, I reckon it's sitting in a box at an antiques shop, waiting to be shipped out to Malcolm De Witt in Paris. That item, a beautiful ceramic bowl, has spent some time stored in a bag of coffee beans – Silver Bullet coffee beans. That means that someone who works for Silver Bullet knows how it got there. Am I right so far?'

Kyle nodded.

'I'm guessing that someone from Silver Bullet stole it during the drinks reception last Friday night after Malcolm told them where it was and how to get in, or Malcolm stole it and handed it over to one of you.'

I gave Kyle a chance to respond, but he didn't take it.

'Is this what you do? Steal when you're travelling the country for food festivals and events?'

'No!' He sounded horrified, then quietly continued, 'Or it wasn't. And it wasn't me. I know about it, but I'm not involved.'

Kyle looked and sounded like he was pleading with me, and I immediately believed him.

'Ben needed money and Guy caught him stealing from a stately home last summer. He threatened to tell the police, but then Ben offered him a cut of any money he got for the item in order to keep him quiet. Guy's all about the money, whatever we're doing, so he said yes and encouraged Ben to steal again. In fact, he started to plan it for him. After that, he made sure that Ben never stole from anywhere we were actually working, only before or after the event so that there was no link.'

'And you knew about it? Why didn't you go to the police?'

Kyle didn't respond and that gave me the few precious moments I needed to fit in another piece of the jigsaw.

'You didn't go to the police because if they investigated, they would likely discover your sham coffee business.' His eyes shot up to meet mine and I nodded. 'I've been to your offices, I know what you're doing: flogging Northern Bean Company coffee as your own and saving yourself all the production costs. I assume that was just a little project to increase your profits, and then it became the perfect cover for stealing artefacts as you travelled for events. Combine the two businesses and the overall profit must be huge.'

Kyle nodded. 'It was so easy. Most of these places have little or no security. Occasionally Guy and Ben would get something of little value, but sometimes they hit the jackpot. Ben was always up for it – he took any chance he could to make some extra money. I managed the coffee side of things to provide the cover and Guy was often down in London, working with Chester to sell whatever Ben managed to steal.'

'Why were you arguing with Guy the other day? It looked pretty nasty.'

'Things changed when Guy started taking orders off people.' I didn't know what he meant and I looked questioningly at him. 'Chester had a couple of clients who were looking for something in particular – an object or painting they knew the owner would never sell – so Chester would arrange a way to get hold of it for them.'

'And that "way" was Ben?' Kyle nodded again. 'The St Ives Bowl, did Malcolm put in a request for that?'

'Yeah, he was at university with the Duke, along with Chester. I reckon he had a chip on his shoulder. He'd made a lot of money, but it was new money. The way he used to talk about their university days made me think he was jealous.'

'And he took something that meant a lot to the Duke to get back at him.' I finished the story off for Kyle. 'So that's what you were fighting over – this was all getting far too serious for you. They'd gone from opportunist thefts to stealing to order and you weren't keen?' Kyle nodded once more. 'And Ben? Did he have a change of heart, threaten to tell the police?'

'Oh hell no, Ben was well up for it. If anything, he didn't think we were doing enough.'

'So why was he killed?'

Kyle shook his head and looked genuinely confused. 'I don't know. Really, I have no idea. Everything was going well. I was here at the pub with Guy the night of the reception and we got a text off Ben to say that he had the bowl and it had all been really easy. As planned, it was stashed in one of the sacks of coffee beans in the van. We figured no one would check there. We'd get it out once the festival was up and running and there were thousands of people to serve as a distraction, and no one would have a clue.'

'What about Guy?'

'What about him? Ben was making him money, so he wouldn't want him gone. And anyway, he was with Malcolm when Ben was killed. I met up with him just before Ben's body was found.'

Despite Kyle's certainty, I wasn't so sure anymore.

'Where's Guy now?'

'Heading back to London. He and Chester had put a couple of jobs on hold until Ben's murder all blew over, but he says he can't wait anymore. Plus I'm not sure Guy wants to get his hands dirty. He was happy leaving that to Ben, so he won't be taking any more orders for a while.'

I drained my glass of coke. 'Are you going to tell the police or am I?'

'What?'

'You can hand yourself in, tell them everything you know and there's a chance they'll look favourably on you. Or you could do a runner and make the whole thing worse.'

I knew he was going to call them; he really didn't seem like the fugitive type. Plus if he was telling the truth, then his involvement wasn't worth being on the run for. I stood up and thanked him for the drink.

'Where are you going?' he asked.

'I think I know what happened, but there's something I need to check out first. I've been barking up the wrong well-manicured tree.'

I sat in the car park at Charleton House and called Joe.

'Sophie, I'm here with your friend, Chester. It appears you've been ignoring my advice.'

'Uh?'

'Well, despite me telling you to keep your nose out, you're clearly still digging for information, so you may as well tell me what else you've got.' He'd made various comments about the need for me to let him do his job, but he'd never taken me aside and torn strips off me, so I figured he couldn't be that annoyed. Plus if what Mark had said about Joe having a thing for me was true, he was unlikely to. I didn't want him to have a thing for me and was trying to forget about it, but on the other hand, if it saved me from a telling off, it might have its uses.

I started to fill him in. 'You're going to have Kyle Rushton contacting you, or at least you should. He said he was going to call.'

'He beat you to it. I had a call on the way here, and he's at the station waiting to talk to me. I presume you know what it's about?'

'I do. You're going to have the thefts all wrapped up by the end of the day. The one thing I'm not so sure about is Ben's murder. I think I know who did it, but you're going to need the help of your Parisian colleagues.'

'I've already put a call in to them,' he responded.

'And Chester? Have you got anything useful from him?'

'He claims to know nothing about the contents of the parcel, that he was just doing someone a favour and shipping it out. He says he has no idea what it is or where it's from.'

'Do you believe him?'

'Of course not. Right now I have a couple of officers going through the other parcels and we've already found the painting from Berwick Hall.'

'And Malcolm?'

'Our Parisian friends will be on their way to apprehend him. Hopefully Chester won't find a way to give him a heads up, so he won't be expecting the knock on his door that's about to come.'

'OK, well, make sure they ask him exactly when Guy was with him. I'm not convinced that either he or Guy have been entirely honest about that morning. I think Guy in particular has a lot of explaining to do.'

'Sure thing, boss. Anything else while I'm at it, or can I go and get on with my job?' Oddly, that question wasn't laden with sarcasm, which slightly threw me off.

'Err, no, I don't think there's any more to tell.'

I could hear voices in the background and someone shouting for Joe. 'I have to go. That's DS Harnby, and if she knows I'm talking to you, she'll kill me. Give me two minutes, I'll call you back.' He hung up.

I'd quite liked Malcolm, he was pleasant company and had seemed harmless enough. But now it seemed he had quite an intense green streak running through him. On the plus side, the Duke would be getting his bowl back. I would be curious to see if it went back on display or if he decided to keep it out of sight; I wouldn't blame him if he did. It seemed his trusting nature had left him a little burnt.

I wasn't going to wait for Joe to call; there was an important conversation I needed to have. I'd got something very badly wrong and I needed to fix it.

I started to walk towards the gardeners' yard.

I found Elliot Forrester in one of the greenhouses. He was tidying up small pots and I was relieved to see that there weren't any sharp objects immediately visible.

He turned as I walked in. 'Oh for crying out loud.' He leant against one of the workbenches that ran along both sides of the narrow building and dropped his head as though he was gathering his energy. 'What do you want?'

I wasn't quite as worried about this conversation as I had been last time we'd spoken, as my motive was very different this time.

'I want you to be honest with me.'

'About what? It's none of your business. If you think I'm a killer, just say so, but you'd have a hard time proving it…'

'Because you didn't kill Ben,' I interrupted. That caught him off guard and he was silent long enough for me to say what I needed to get out. 'I don't believe you did it, but there's enough evidence to make people think you did. If you tell the truth it will be easier for everyone else to believe you too.'

'This isn't anyone's business.'

'But you've made it people's business by having a go at Ben in public. You've put the idea out there. Elliot, you must know you have a reputation for having a bit of a temper. It makes people wonder whether you could go further – or at least, it did after some of us saw you with Ben last week.'

He grunted in response, but I took it as some sort of acquiescence.

'It's private,' he said quietly. 'Private, that's all.'

Now I had a second man in front of me who appeared defeated. Elliot was such a big, muscular man that it seemed even more incongruous than it had with Kyle. He clearly had the strength to do some real harm – throw me over his shoulder and bury my body, but with his slouched shoulders and downcast eyes, he looked as if someone had found a nozzle and let the air out of him.

He looked up at me. 'I hated him, but I didn't want him dead. I just wanted him to clear off and leave us alone. I told him to time and time again, but he was always sending money. Lots of it. I'm a damned good father, I can provide for my family. I didn't need his help, but he wouldn't stop. It was embarrassing.'

I spoke softly; I didn't want to antagonise him. 'He's Isabella's father?'

'*I'm* her father,' he spat back. 'I've raised her, provided for her. I'm the one that she calls Dad, not him.'

'But he's her biological father?'

He stared hard at the floor, then slowly nodded. 'But that's all. He promised me he'd stay away, they both promised me they'd have nothing more to do with each other, and Carla and I would raise Isabella as our own. But he kept sending money; he told us he'd set up a savings account to send her to college. The idiot was getting into more and more debt doing it. It was as though he was trying to prove a point, make up for sleeping with Carla by throwing money at Isabella, but he was making it worse.

'Look, I'm not happy he's dead. I'm not heartless. I guess he loved his daughter, but I didn't want him round here. It turned out I had already shared Carla with him, I didn't want to share my daughter with him as well.'

'And then he arrived at the food festival. That must have been hard.'

'I couldn't believe it, I was furious. That was why I had a go at him. I know it was stupid, but you've no idea how hard it is. I'm not an idiot; I know a lot of people round here know about him and Carla and what they did, and I have to live with that every day that I come into work. But he was just rubbing my face in it. I lost it. It was stupid.'

'And the next morning? I know there was a period of time when Robin left you alone. There was time for you to go and kill him.'

'I know that now, but I don't know what I can do about it. I just stayed in the Rock Garden, working; I never left, I swear.'

For the first time, Elliot looked as if he needed something from me. He had a temper, but I felt sorry for him. Imagine knowing that everyone around you was aware of your private life and were all just playing along. There was a child-sized elephant in the room every day of his life. I knew that the last thing he wanted was pity, but that was what I felt.

'I believe you.'

His whole body relaxed and he lifted his face up to the roof. With his eyes closed, he asked, 'What do I need to do?'

'Nothing, Elliot, not right now. I think that while we've been talking, a few things have been sorting themselves out. I need to make a phone call. The police might still want to talk to you, confirm a few things, but if what I'm thinking is right, then you don't need to worry.'

He didn't respond. His eyes met mine again and I smiled. There was nothing left to say, so I turned and walked out of the greenhouse. I needed to get out into the fresh air; I'd spent a week believing that an innocent man had killed someone and I felt dreadful.

. . .

I took a long route through the gardens. There was no sign of the festival and its little white tents. All the cables had been packed away, the gravel raked over so there was no evidence of the cars and trucks that had removed all the stallholders and their goods from the site. The ducks were happily doing laps around the pond and the flowerbeds once again took pride of place. There was no indication that thousands of people had been enjoying pork pies or fudge, cider or freshly made lemonade right here just a few days ago.

There was also no sign that someone had been murdered here less than a week ago, twenty feet from where I was standing.

After giving myself time to take a few deep breaths, I walked back to the Library Café. I felt like I'd been neglecting my team over the last couple of days, and the least I could do was help them clear up and close for the day. I reached the entrance to the café and pushed the door open.

'Sophie?' I jumped, my hand flew to my chest and I stopped breathing for a moment. I felt like I'd returned to the first day of the festival when Guy had surprised me, spilling my coffee. At least this time I didn't have hot liquid in my hand.

'What the hell...'

Chelsea was standing immediately behind the door, chewing hard on a piece of gum and apparently waiting for me. She went bright red.

'Sorry, I thought you'd seen me.'

'Chelsea, what have I told you before?'

'Eh?'

'Chewing gum, Chelsea, get rid of it.'

She looked around and grabbed a napkin off a table, spitting the offending lump into it. 'You had a phone call. Bruce Keen, and he sounded desperate to talk to you. I told him you'd call him back.'

I took the slip of paper that Chelsea passed to me, Bruce's number scrawled on it, and put it in my pocket. He could wait until tomorrow morning. Right now, clearing dirty plates and wiping down tables seemed like the most normal thing I could possibly do, and I needed some normality back in my life.

CHAPTER 17

For the first time in weeks, there were grey clouds overhead and, if I'm honest, I was overjoyed. Like anyone else, I spend the British winter longing for spring to arrive, and then I start pining for summer to come, and with it the chance to leave the house without a coat (not without picking it up and putting it down a dozen times first, of course). But after the recent weeks of high temperatures, I was happy for some respite. My office was still unbearable – the thick old walls of Charleton House did a great job of holding in the heat, but at least it was now possible to sit in almost any seat in the cafés and not stick to the furniture.

I had decided that it was time for a change and so, at nine-thirty in the morning, before the visitors arrived on what promised to be a busy Saturday, Joe and Mark joined me for coffee in the Garden Café.

'I'm not sure whether I should be flattered or deeply suspicious,' Mark commented as he eyed me over the miniature glass flower vase and perfectly laid-out silver cutlery. 'I haven't been invited out anywhere with tablecloths since... ooh, since Bill was still trying to woo me, which was fifteen years ago.' He thought for a moment. 'I'm going to have words with him, he needs to step up his game. I'm quite a catch and he shouldn't forget it. I deserve a few more classy restaurants in my life.'

I sniggered, but straightened my face out as much as I could when he caught me. The glare that followed could have shattered the glass vase, if it hadn't been combined with Mark sticking his tongue out.

Joe was back in his motorcycle leathers and they creaked as he made himself comfortable. A server in a crisp white shirt with the Ravensbury ducal coronet embroidered on the pocket made his way over. He was carrying a tray with a large French press and three china cups. The cups were beautifully decorated with views of the estate. The server smiled at me as he placed one with a scene that included a herd of deer on it in front of me; it seemed my love of the beasts was becoming well known. Appallingly, I didn't know his name; I would have to change that and let his supervisor know I was impressed at the rather classy example of sucking up to the boss. I was also going to remind his supervisor that he should have been wearing a name badge: one hand giveth, the other taketh away, or something like that.

As Mark poured our coffees, I pulled out a notebook. I'd spent the previous night pulling together all my thoughts, trying to see if I could fill some of the gaps before Joe did, but as he had a couple of suspects in custody and the Paris gendarmerie had, I presumed, Malcolm in a cell on the other side of the Channel, I was sure to be less well-informed than he.

Joe turned to me. 'As you insist on getting involved, no matter what I say, you go first. I'll tell you if you stray off the path.'

'And don't miss anything out,' Mark added. 'I know you two have already spoken to one another, but I'm just as important a member of the three musketeers.'

I looked at Joe, who subtly raised his hands in a 'no idea' way. I decided not to comment.

'OK, so there are three things going on here. In the background there are the thefts from numerous historic houses around the country, all of which are open to the public. There's Ben's murder, and then there's the shady business dealings of Silver Bullet Coffee.'

Talking of coffee, I took a mouthful. It was far too bitter.

'Silver Bullet Coffee are selling themselves as a Derbyshire-based coffee-roasting company. They appear at a lot of the food festivals in the county and beyond, supply a few shops and have enough of a reputation that people recognise them, know them to talk to and view them as a legitimate business that roasts reasonably good coffee. They certainly started out that way, renting equipment at a roasting facility, probably because they were a start-up business and couldn't afford their own equipment.

'Ben, who I'll come to in detail later, was always trying to get more money, and on a whim stole something from one of the historical houses that was holding an event they were working at. Guy finds out and threatens to blow the whistle on him unless Ben gives him a cut of the profits, and thus a new business is born. Am I right so far?'

Joe nodded.

Our server made a perfectly timed return and placed a plate piled high with miniature pastries in front of us. They were fresh and still warm from the oven. I smiled at him and passed him the empty French press, hoping he'd realise that we needed it refilling. Joe took over the story while Mark inhaled a mini chocolate croissant.

'Guy is claiming he had no idea and it was all Ben...'

'You have Guy? Since when?'

'Since late last night. Sadly he was too far ahead for us to catch him down in London, but we made an educated guess that he'd try and make the most of his contact in Paris. He was identified on a boat from Dover and picked up by the gendarmerie when they docked in Calais. He claimed he had business in Paris.

What he didn't realise was that his "business" was in a Parisian police cell.'

'So you have Malcolm too?'

'We can function reasonably well without your help,' Joe replied.

I removed the apricot Danish pastry that he was holding from his fingers as a response and took an enormous bite before muttering, 'And?'

Joe playfully shook his head. 'And he's singing like a canary.'

That didn't surprise me; I didn't really imagine Malcolm having a backbone of steel.

'Can I finish?' Joe asked. I nodded and reached for another pastry, a chocolate twist this time.

'Ben approached Chester to sell on the first few antiques he'd stolen and got lucky. Chester has been involved in dodgy deals for years, but we've never been able to pin anything on him. He recognised an opportunity when he saw one and had enough contacts on the antiques black market that he could get rid of the items Ben took, while taking a percentage of the profits of course.'

I took over while Joe reached for another pastry. 'At this point, when Guy got involved and he and Ben started to make decent money – albeit in a criminal fashion – most coffee roasters would have invested in their own equipment. But not Silver Bullet. They started repackaging coffee roasted by the Northern Bean Company, saving themselves money, but also making life easy for themselves when the company became just a front. They didn't want to be making too much of an effort; coffee's not what they really cared about. It might have been in the beginning, but not now. Instead, Guy used one of his first big payments to buy the Airstream. It gave them an air of success and looked great, so they were invited to more and more events and they had more access to buildings with valuable treasures.'

This, of course, had added Bruce Keen into the mix.

'Did you talk to Bruce?' I asked Joe.

'I did, and I don't think I've met someone quite so nervous, despite being completely innocent. He was babbling like a schoolkid who was being wrongly accused of stealing someone's lunch money. It took me forever to get him to calm down enough for me to understand what he was saying.

'Like you, he was just passing the estate where Silver Bullet had its premises and dropped in to say hello and check out where they were based. He'd met the guys plenty of times before, but they'd always engineered things so any meetings were held away from their offices, understandably. But they hadn't planned on him dropping by unannounced. When he saw what they were doing, he was furious. He must have accidentally dropped his card while he was there. He got to Charleton House early on Saturday morning to confront them, and a friend who had one of the stalls got him in. He couldn't see any activity over at the Airstream so assumed no one was in there, and didn't get his chance to talk to Guy or Kyle before the body was found. He knew that he had motive and opportunity and has spent the week absolutely terrified.'

No wonder Bruce had been furious and wanted to rearrange our meeting on the Friday – he'd just discovered what the Silver Bullet lads were up to. I felt sorry for him, but not enough to stop me ditching his coffee. I had my standards.

'But why did they take the Duke's fruit bowl if it's of no financial value to anyone?' asked Mark as he topped up everyone's mugs from the newly returned French press.

'As you well know, that fruit bowl, as you call it, was hand-crafted by one of the finest ceramicists of the twentieth century, who was also a very close friend of the Duke's mother, the late Dowager Duchess. It has no financial value, but the sentimental value is huge.'

Mark pretended to look apologetic, but then I had done my

finest impression of a well-spoken headmistress who was disappointed in his ignorance. I continued.

'Malcolm went to university with the Duke, and although they got on pretty well at the time and were part of the same social circle, Malcolm still ended up with an enormous chip on his shoulder. One that he carries with him to this day. The Duke was extremely wealthy, as were most of his friends, and Malcolm was from a regular working background and couldn't compete. He knew all about the bowl; in fact, there's every chance he met the artist. He was spending summers here at Charleton House around the same time that she became part of the Dowager Duchess's social scene.

'After running into the Duke at a university reunion a couple of months back, and having his chip deepened, Malcolm came up with a way of getting his own back. Chester had been a fellow student and was also at the reunion. I'm guessing that over a few too many glasses of port, Chester and Malcolm came up with a plan. Chester could put him in touch with Guy, who was by that point running the whole Silver Bullet artefacts stealing operation, and arrange for the bowl to be taken. In return, Malcolm, who isn't short of a penny or two – self-made, of course – could pay them good money. The reception last Friday night was the perfect opportunity. Malcolm could feed information to Ben, Ben could use that information to steal the bowl without being seen, and then...'

I looked at Joe. I had my suspicions as to what had happened next, but I hoped he and his colleagues, both here and in France, had been able to gather enough information to confirm my idea. I was about to share my theory when the empty chair next to me was scraped back and a cloud of mint green and lavender settled down. Joyce had joined us, resembling one of the beds in the garden. I half expected a swarm of bees to be following close behind.

'Good morning, how are we all?' She looked around the table. 'Am I interrupting something?'

'Sophie was just about to tell us who killed Ben,' chipped in Mark, allowing Joyce to catch up in record speed.

'Oh my God, poor Ben, you know who did it? I don't care what he got mixed up in, but the sweet young boy that I remember did not deserve to be killed.'

Our nameless server had returned with a cup for Joyce and poured her some coffee. I watched as Joyce picked up the cup; her nails had been painted in stripes that matched her outfit and were long enough to be used to stir in the lumps of sugar she'd added. I forced myself to focus as it looked as if everyone was waiting for me to carry on.

'It's not that complicated, I just got side-tracked by Elliot Forrester. His display of anger, his history with Ben, Isabella's paternity – it all made perfect sense that he might want to kill Ben in a fit of pique, and so I focused on him as the most likely killer. I'd accepted that as he was a friend of the Duke, Malcolm's alibi was going to be unquestionable, and as a result Guy had a rock-solid alibi too. But I was wrong, wasn't I?' I looked at Joe.

'As much as I hate to say it, Sophie, you were. Guy did join Malcolm, but not for as long as they claimed. Guy had gone to the Silver Bullet van on the Saturday morning to meet Ben and retrieve the bowl that had been safely hidden in one of the sacks of coffee beans. We worked this out from all the information you gathered, Sophie – thank you, by the way.' He placed his hand on mine briefly and I saw that Mark had spotted it. That was all I needed.

Joe continued, 'Ben was keen to save as much money as possible. Every chance to make any extra cash, he took it. When Guy turned up, they got into an argument about money. Ben wanted more – a lot more – and Guy wasn't having any of it. They got into a fight, and in the process, Guy grabbed the... you know, the coffee thing?'

'Portafilter.'

'Portafilter, and hit him with it. He didn't have to worry about fingerprints as he had good reason for them to be all over the van, so he tried to make it look like a burglary gone wrong, took some of the stock, and then called Malcolm who snuck him into his room. Once there, Guy made him agree to provide an alibi or he'd reveal Malcolm's plan to steal from the Duke. Guy's claiming that it was self-defence, that Ben got angry when he refused to increase his cut and Guy was afraid he was going to be killed.'

Joyce shook her head. 'All because he loved his daughter.'

'Who, the gardener? But he didn't do it.' Now Mark was looking confused, so I topped up his coffee. He clearly needed it. On the other hand, and despite having been at the table for only two minutes, Joyce had caught up and enlightened him.

'Mark, if you spent as much time listening to people as you spend sculpting your moustache, you'd know that I meant Ben. He made a huge mistake when he slept with Carla years ago and took a back seat in raising Isabella. But she was his daughter and his love for her, combined with a need to make up for his mistakes, led to him throwing money at her. That in due course led to him making some rather silly mistakes, which led to his death.'

'So what happens now?' I asked.

'We finish off the interviews, and the Art and Antiques Unit will come in to help us try and track all the objects that have been stolen over the last twelve months. There's also a chance that they'll be able to find evidence of more of Chester's black market dealings while they're at it.'

'It's Elliot I feel sorry for.' We all turned to face Mark, who seemed to be having a rare introspective moment. He looked up at the three of us. 'What? The poor guy's private life is already a non-secret round here. This will have blown it further out into the open. Everyone knows he was a suspect; he's been one of the water-cooler topics for days. I'm sure he just wants to put what Carla did behind him and get on with his life.'

'He won't need to worry about it for long,' said Joyce. 'I heard that he resigned first thing this morning. Came in at six o'clock, gave his month's notice and asked to be given duties that took him as far away from the house and the rest of the staff as possible.'

'What will he do?' Joe asked. Joyce shrugged.

'There's plenty of grand gardens that need staff in Derbyshire. Some are open to the public, some not, but either way he'll have no problem getting work. I was always surprised that he hadn't left before, but the gossip had died down and he just got on with his job. He never socialised with his colleagues, not after Carla... well, you know.'

'You could always transfer from retail to gardens and replace him,' Mark suggested.

'What?' Joyce responded, her voice dripping with incredulity.

'Well, you look the part. You could be a roving lavender display, attracting bees and wildlife to different parts of the garden.'

I put my head in my hands. Joyce's nails, or talons, could easily be used as weapons and Mark was sitting dangerously close to her. I worried for his safety.

'Young man, I like Sophie a great deal. For unknown reasons, she has become extremely fond of you, so for her sake alone I will suffer from a brief moment of partial deafness and assume that what I just heard was no more than a rather embarrassing bout of flatulence.' As I raised my head, she slowly brought her cup to her lips and stared at Mark as she took a long sip of coffee. Her eyes never left him, even as she placed her cup perfectly in the centre of the saucer. If I hadn't known Joyce any better, I would have been terrified.

'Well, I owe you all a great deal of thanks.' Joe raised his cup in the air. He spoke quickly and glanced in my direction, but I knew he was trying to save Mark from himself. In a battle of wits between him and Joyce, there was no guarantee that Mark would win. 'Sophie in particular. I've always known you had an unhealthy coffee addiction, but I would never have thought that it would help solve a case. You are a wonderful addition to the Charleton House clan.'

'Hear, hear,' chimed Joyce and Mark, their momentary clash forgotten.

'You know, she could be worse.' Mark had taken on a considered tone, which meant that he had entered tour guide mode and was about to enlighten us. 'Rumour has it that Beethoven counted out his coffee beans each morning to ensure that each cup of coffee was to his taste. He required precisely sixty beans.' He raised his eyebrows at us, then buried his face back in his cup. We were silent. It was a 'mic-drop' moment.

Joe broke the silence. 'She looks like a sixty-five bean girl to me.' He locked eyes with me over his coffee cup and I prayed that I wouldn't see any twinkling. I desperately tried to think of something to say, but ironically, I didn't seem to have had enough coffee to think that quickly.

'Well, if you've finished solving murders and identifying coffee scandals, I have places to be, tours to give, stories to tell.' Mark got up from the table. I could have hugged him for his timing. 'Sophie, I'll see you later for a celebratory gin in the Black Swan. Joe, I expect you to be there. Joyce,' – he paused briefly – 'you are a visual delight and I adore you. There will be a glass of prosecco with your name on it should you wish to grace us with your presence.' He kissed her on the cheek and walked away quickly enough that she couldn't have reached for him if she'd tried.

Joe and I sat in nervous silence.

'Oh, for heaven's sake!' Joyce exclaimed, taking in our anxious faces. 'He's a fool, but my life would be much less colourful without him in it.'

'I doubt it,' risked Joe, looking her dress up and down. All three of us laughed as Joyce put her cup down and picked up her handbag. It was large enough to constitute a sack and had an enormous image of a peacock feather printed on the side.

'Sophie, dear, I believe we are expected somewhere.'

She was right. I had come to an agreement with Signal Box Coffee that Lucy and Kathy would supply some of the coffee we used at the house. Sadly, they were unable to produce the quantities I needed to supply all our cafés, so we'd decided that theirs would be the special blend that was served in the Garden Café and at events. Joyce and I were off to meet with them and discuss selling bags of the same blend, and maybe a few others roasted especially for Charleton House, in the gift shops.

I'd been at Charleton House for just over twelve months and I was going to finally start putting my mark on the cafés. I had all sorts of plans to give them real personality and a solid connection with the house, its history and the stories that inhabited its walls. So long as there were no more murders for me to become distracted by, I could make a lot happen here.

Joyce looked over her shoulder. 'Come on, Sophie, chop-chop.'

'No more murders,' I said under my breath. Now there was a phrase I never thought I'd hear myself use.

READ THE FIRST CHARLETON HOUSE MYSTERY

Building a relationship with my readers is one of the best things about writing. I occasionally send newsletters with details on new releases, special offers, interviews and articles relating to The Charleton House Mysteries.

Sign up to my mailing list and you'll also receive the very first Charleton House Mystery, *A Stately Murder.*

Head to my website for your free copy and find out what happens when Sophie stumbles across the victim of the first murder Charleton House has ever known.

www.katepadams.com

ABOUT THE AUTHOR

After 25 years working in some of England's finest buildings, Kate P. Adams has turned to murder.

Kate grew up in Derbyshire, the setting for the Charleton House Mysteries, and went on to work in theatres around the country, the Natural History Museum - London, the University of Oxford and Hampton Court Palace. Every day she explored darkened corridors and rooms full of history behind doors the public never get to enter. Kate spent years in these beautiful buildings listening to fantastic tales, wondering where the bodies were hidden, and hoping that she'd run into a ghost or two.

Kate has an unhealthy obsession with finding the perfect cup of coffee, enjoys a gin and tonic, and is managed by Pumpkin, a domineering tabby cat who is a little on the large side. Now that she lives in the USA, writing the Charleton House Mysteries allows Kate to go home to her beloved Derbyshire every day, in her head at least.

ACKNOWLEDGEMENTS

Just as it takes a dedicated team to run a historic house, it takes a team to bring a book out into the world. I am lucky enough to have a fabulous, generous and extremely knowledgeable team of my own.

Thank you to my wonderful beta readers Chris Bailey-Jones, Elin Begley, Joanna Hancox, Lynne McCormack, Eileen Minchin, Rosanna Summers. Your honesty and insightful comments keep me on the straight and narrow.

I have always wanted to ensure that life in a historic house that is open to the public is portrayed as accurately as possible. I can bring my own twenty-year career in visitor experience to bear on this. However I have needed the expertise of those who work in specialist fields. My thanks to Kerren Harris - conservation, Rosanna Summers– live interpretation, Aileen Peirce - access to historical information, Mark Wallis – live interpretation and historical costume, Liz Young – event management. It was great working with you all again. Any errors are mine, not theirs.

Richard Mason, my police advisor who guides me on procedure and makes sure I am, largely, within the law. When I break the rules, that's all me!

My fabulous editor, Alison Jack, and Julia Gibbs my eagle-eyed proofreader. Both are a joy to work with.

Thank you to Susan Stark, whose constant encouragement means that I keep sitting at my computer, and finding out what Sophie, Mark and Joyce are getting up to.

There is, in Scotland, a historic house called Charleton that bears no similarities to my own. Many thanks to its owner, Baron St Clair Bonde, who was happy for me to use the name. I am extremely grateful to him.